CODENAME: ROCKSTAR

CODENAME: ROCKSTAR

SPELLBOUND SECURITY™
BOOK ONE

TR CAMERON   MARTHA CARR   MICHAEL ANDERLE

DON'T MISS OUR NEW RELEASES

Join the LMBPN email list to be notified of new releases and special promotions (which happen often) by following this link:

http://lmbpn.com/email/

Copyright © 2024 LMBPN Publishing
Cover by Fantasy Book Design
Cover copyright © LMBPN Publishing
A Michael Anderle Production

LMBPN Publishing
2375 E. Tropicana Avenue, Suite 8-305
Las Vegas, Nevada 89119 USA

Version 1.00, November 2024
ebook ISBN: 979-8-89354-342-1
Print ISBN: 979-8-89354-406-0

THE CODENAME: ROCKSTAR TEAM

Thanks to our Beta Readers:
Sean Kesterson
Dorothy Lloyd
Dave Hicks
Zacc Pelter
Diane L. Smith
Jeff Goode
Christopher Gilliard
Wendy L Bonell
Peter Manis
Jackey Hankard-Brodie
Jan Hunnicutt

Thanks to our JIT Readers:

Editor
SkyFyre Editing Team

CHAPTER ONE

Danica Grey stood with her back against the wall at one end of a large, rectangular room. The white-painted walls all around featured enormous oil canvases featuring images of places where land met ocean. A lectern stood on a raised stage to her right, waiting for whatever notable would proclaim from it. A veritable sea of round tables filled the rest of the room, appropriate to the imagery of the paintings.

What was probably the hotel's biggest room was full of men in tuxedos and bow ties accompanied by women in beautiful gowns with elaborate hairdos. She didn't fit in among this gaggle of well-to-do quad- and penta-generians.

Someone who took note of her would first see the off-white suit and matching pumps, offset by a soft gray blouse. Next, they'd take in her long blonde hair and the perfectly smooth skin that her practiced and adept use of makeup provided. Her nails were shaped and polished in a deep red that matched her lipstick and stood out against the rest of the outfit. The darker color was her little piece of originality. She laughed inwardly. *Yeah, I'm a total rebel.*

If someone were to stand beside her, they might notice the small object nestled in her slightly pointed left ear. Its body was clear, but the electronics inside were silver, black, and odd-looking in that spot. No one was likely to get that close tonight since she was part of the surroundings, not a participant in the main event.

Perfectly clear speech came through the earpiece, easily overcoming the chatter and conversations of the guests as Arthur Blackwood's cultured British voice ordered, "Report."

Danica's gaze tracked around the room and briefly settled on each of Spellbound Security's guards as they reported. Her role was to be strictly an observer after accepting Arthur's request to observe his team in action and provide feedback on their performance.

Six guards were along the walls, two at the back, two on the far side, and two holding position on her wall. She couldn't see those responsible for the next round of responses, which came from personnel in the corridors surrounding the big room. The last two guards, a tuxedoed man and a gowned woman sitting at a table with their protectees, gave natural-seeming nods instead of verbal responses to indicate their awareness.

Arthur said, "Good. The event kicks off in ten minutes, they tell me. Keep your eyes and ears open, people."

Danica swept her gaze across the room methodically, left to right in the near section, the opposite in the middle, and the same in the far section, before repeating it in reverse. The Spellbound Security personnel wore dark glasses that would have information projected on them from the team's technical support. She hadn't received a pair since her role was to watch the guards, not the data, although she wondered how Arthur had explained her status to the others.

The members of Spellbound Security Miami didn't know she was there to evaluate them. Arthur had introduced her as a consultant for the hotel, which was considering giving them a long-term contract. Spellbound was already well respected, with offices in New York, Los Angeles, and Miami, although their work took them far beyond those three cities. This event was at a beachside resort in Tampa, Florida.

Danica laughed inwardly. It had been *very* easy to accept the offer of a free trip to Tampa for the weekend in return for providing one night's observation and a formal report with recommendations. The company she worked for, Castle Investigations, was unaware of her moonlighting, but nothing in her contract prohibited it.

She had put in her required hours at work for the week before coming to Tampa and would be back in plenty of time to get in on Monday, although whether she managed to sleep beforehand was another question entirely. The nightlife in Tampa was supposed to be something special, and the resort hotel had a beach party every night that she'd heard was wild, crazy, and fun. Danica wasn't one to turn down any of those things.

Arthur warned, "Five minutes."

His accent always made her smile. Her family had met him in Europe during the time they'd moved from one military base to the next to the next to support her father's career. Their connection had continued in the decades since, and he'd put in a good word for her with her current employers.

She would have done this gig for nothing if he'd asked because he was essentially family. She wasn't about to turn down a paycheck, either. She was loyal, not stupid.

Her routine scanning of the room stopped as the entrance doors were closed and black-uniformed servers moved through the crowd to deliver appetizers. A speaker stepped up onto the stage and began to talk. Danica processed the sight in an instant, noting that it was a woman dressed in a sharp business suit with an American flag pin on her lapel.

Her mind categorized the woman as a politician and immediately put thoughts of her aside. It was unlikely that the governor, senator, representative, or whatever the woman was would be a threat to the board of trustees of Coralsyne Corporation, which had hired Spellbound Security for protection.

Arthur had explained that an infomancer broke into the company's servers and accessed the calendars of its executives and trustees before the company's countermeasures could eject the intruder. The breach had alarmed Coralsyne enough to hire extra protection for this event. Their security personnel were also onsite but not operating in conjunction with Spellbound beyond a shared radio channel.

A bored male voice reported in her earpiece, "Nothing on the cameras. This place is pretty buttoned up."

One of the guards on her side of the room muttered, "Must be tough, sitting up there in a plush hotel room watching television. I bet you're wearing the free robe, too."

The technician laughed. "Someone's got to do the dirty work, right? We can't all have the glory positions. I noticed a lot of pretty women's eyes turning your way, though."

Danica suppressed a smile at the banter and resumed sweeping the room with her gaze.

Some operations she'd been part of would have slammed down such small talk, but Arthur's philosophy was to hire the best people he could and let them do their jobs without harassment. If that meant a little levity while everyone was doing their jobs, he didn't see it as a problem. She didn't either, although she had the benefit of not being responsible for the evening's outcome. If she was, she supposed she might feel differently.

She began a slow circuit of the room to evaluate the positioning and attentiveness of the other guards. Her gaze continued to rove in search of threats, although she doubted any would materialize.

Danica wasn't sure who would want to take out a board of trustees unless it was a corporate competitor. Kidnapping or whatever seemed a bit much for business types. Still, people did things for reasons she couldn't comprehend all the time, so she wasn't about to eliminate it as a possibility.

She had made it halfway around the room when she got a familiar itch where her spine met her skull. Danica had elven blood deep in her family tree. The magical abilities that came with the bloodline were weak in some generations and strong in others. She was one of the strongest magicals in her family's recent memory, and one of her naturally active abilities was an enhanced sense of the presence of magic.

The realization that magic was nearby manifested in different ways, sometimes as a taste, sometimes a smell, and sometimes the creepy crawlies she got on the back of her neck. She warned, "Eyes up. Active magic in the room." It was a bit of an overstatement. She wasn't positive it was in the room, only that it was nearby.

Arthur replied, "Could you be detecting cosmetic illusions or things like that? This is a crowd that would use them."

Danica's lips twitched in annoyance because she couldn't rule it out. "It's possible, but this feels stronger than those usually do."

Many people in the modern era used magic, whether theirs or purchased from others, for simple cosmetic changes. Changing one's hair color for a night was a popular one. Everyone who had entered had walked through a hidden scanner, which meant no strong magic was present. None of that explained the increasing feeling of magic use.

As Danica resumed her slow patrol around the room, her gaze drifted to the pair of Spellbound Security employees seated at the table with the board members. They were older than the rest of the Spellbound Security personnel, in their late forties, and thus fit in better with the assembled group than the others could. Danica was closer to the average Spellbound age at twenty-eight, although she was still older than several guards watching the corridors.

She stopped moving and squinted. Right *there*, beyond

the table with the trustees and the guards. Something was wrong. It was like wearing glasses with a tiny bit of grease on them, which distorted the vision barely a touch at the edge of notice. She snapped, "At least one veil in the room, near our table."

Arthur snapped, "Get them out."

No sooner had the guards along the walls begun to move toward the table than six enemies appeared around it, each wearing tuxedos and masks and holding pistols pointed at the ceiling.

She'd been wrong. Big businesses played rougher than she thought. Danica growled a curse as instinct propelled her to dash toward the table.

CHAPTER TWO

Danica automatically reached back for the gun normally holstered at the base of her spine but came up with nothing. She wasn't licensed in the state, and although Spellbound Security's connections with law enforcement were probably wide enough to encompass her, she hadn't wanted to risk getting caught. Apart from the two Spellbound Security agents at the table, she was the protector nearest to the action but was still too far away to engage.

Impressively, the pair embedded with the trustees had snapped into motion almost instantly. Each had moved to grapple with the attacker nearest them. The fact that no shots rang out indicated that the enemy hadn't been aware of their presence and thus hadn't expected such a fast reaction.

Danica hoped the Spellbound Security agents had body armor under their fancy clothes for when the enemy got their act together. She decided that getting rid of the weapons had to be her priority.

She extended her magic with a delicate touch, using force magic like telekinesis to turn the nearest gun to the perfect angle that would allow her to rip it from the attacker's grasp. Once it was free, she hurled it across the room onto the vacant stage, away from where security herded the politician out a far door. The attackers recovered from their initial surprise, and three grabbed tuxedoed men by their collars and pulled them away from the table and down to the floor.

Time seemed to slow as things played out, as often happened in such moments. The one whose pistol she'd stolen reached into his jacket for something else as he processed what had happened. The tuxedoed Spellbound agent had been knocked to the floor, and Danica's eye caught the moment when the female agent landed a kick to her opponent's midsection that dropped him to the floor in agony.

The chaotic motions of the people involved made inserting magic into the fight difficult, but she still had her eyes locked on the one she'd disarmed. He was far enough away from the others to present a clean target. She thrust a fist forward and barked a command word as she imagined a force fist crossing the room to slam into her target. At her imagined impact, he flipped backward as her magical uppercut slammed into his jaw. He was out of the fight for the moment.

Danica used force magic to wrap the trustees thrown to the floor in shields to protect them from whatever immediate danger threatened them. The barriers would diminish the blows of fists and feet and also prevent standard bullets from penetrating. At first look, the attackers didn't seem sophisticated enough to carry anti-magic rounds, but one could never be sure.

As she barreled forward, she used her magic to slap pistols out of more hands and sent them flying toward the stage. She leapt onto the table a moment later and threw herself at the nearest unengaged opponent.

Danica had been a gymnast and a martial artist during her childhood and continued practicing the latter in the present day. It was natural for her to somersault in midair and come down ready for a kick. She pistoned her leg into the chest of one of the bad guys and sent him flying backward to land on another table, which collapsed beneath him. The blow absorbed most of her momentum. She dropped cleanly to the floor in perfect balance, then spun into a back kick aimed at the next nearest.

Unfortunately, it didn't take him by surprise, and he also had some skills. He stepped back, raised one arm to block, and used the other to grab her ankle and violently twist it. She leapt into a spin that went with the motion and brought her free foot around to smack into the back of his head. The blow lacked force, but the motion broke his hold. He backed away as she hit the floor on her toes and palms, then bounced back up.

A punch slammed into the thin shield covering her body. She only had a single layer active due to using her magic for other purposes. Her jaw ached from the blow, and she judged that it might've rendered her unconscious without the magical protection.

Her foe shook his hand, scowled at her, and tried another punch. Danica batted it aside and stepped inside his guard. Her hand slammed down toward his groin. He twisted to protect it, and she struck his thigh, then reversed the swing back up into his face. He knocked that one aside enough to take it on the cheekbone rather than square on his nose, but the blow still distracted him.

Danica twisted for torque and slammed an elbow into his solar plexus. He gasped and went down at the same time as the opponent facing the tuxedoed Spellbound agent. She turned a quick circle to look for threats and saw a familiar hazy distortion moving toward the far door. She snapped, "Veiled figure, heading for north exit from the ballroom," and ran after the haze as it left the room. With people in the way, she jumped onto a nearby table, accidentally kicked a plate across the room as she skidded for a moment, and leapt over a seeming sea of cowering guests.

She landed with too much momentum and slammed into the wall, then redirected herself in pursuit. Whatever Spellbound agent had been guarding the corridor must've entered the ballroom when things started to happen because the only ones in the hallway were panicked people pressed against the walls or falling to the floor. The haze was moving fast ahead of her, and she figured it was using a force shield as a battering ram to clear its path.

Well, force magic was handy for all kinds of things. Danica extended her hand to a fire extinguisher on the wall and whipped her arm forward to rip the object from its brackets and hurl it down the conveniently cleared hallway at head height. It struck the hazy spot and dropped with a metallic *thunk* on the tile.

She snarled, "Shielded. Damn competent enemies." The visual aberration turned a corner as she tossed a nearby trash can at it, and as she whipped around the angle in pursuit, she dropped with a yelp to dodge the fire extinguisher that zipped over her head to slam into the wall.

She shouted, "Bastard, quit stealing my moves," popped back up, and threw a fist-sized fireball at an exposed sprinkler head in the ceiling. Water gushed down and revealed the shape of the shield protecting the running figure. Her opponent canceled the useless veil as he spun and threw shadow magic at her.

Danica created force discs on her fists to intercept the attack. She disliked the purple power, which always made her feel queasy. She knew how to use it and would if necessary, but it wasn't her first choice. Unlike her foe.

When that attack failed, her opponent switched to ice and blasted a cone of frost at her. It froze when it hit the falling water and continued flying at her. She created a force wedge in front of her to deflect the attack as she ran at the man. He turned the water at her feet to ice, and she slid for several feet, cursing her footwear under her breath, before regaining her balance to discover he was rabbiting again.

Danica reached out for the fallen fire extinguisher, lifted it from the floor with her force magic, then barked a sharp curse as it fell. Someone had activated an anti-magic emitter, and she was as bereft of magic as any non-magical. She gritted her teeth and raced after her foe. This was one of the reasons she'd kept up her martial arts training beyond a love of it. Sometimes magic wouldn't solve her problems.

She turned another corner and jumped to avoid a metal shelf her enemy had toppled as they passed, then leapt over a cart of trays her enemy had tipped over. She got a better look at him now with no shields, veils, or shadow magic to block separating them. He had long and straight black hair and wore a tuxedo. He wasn't masked as the others had been, which she took for overconfidence in his magical concealment. Since all she could see was the back of his head, it did her little good.

A guard she recognized from the Spellbound Security meeting before the event appeared from around the corner ahead of them. She shouted a warning, but it was already too late. As her ally scrabbled for the pistol at his belt, the man running in front of her drew a gun and fired. Three rounds struck the guard in the chest, and he went down.

Danica slid to her knees beside him and quickly checked him over. He was breathing steadily, although shocked, and no blood came through his shirt. She touched it and felt the ballistic material underneath.

"You'll be okay. Sorry for this." She rolled him over, pulled the anti-magic emitter backpack he was wearing from his back and the pistol from his hand, then ran after her foe.

Danica caught sight of him again as he entered a huge industrial kitchen. Magic flicked back unexpectedly, and she summoned shields layered upon her in time to deflect the frying pan that flew at her head with a protected forearm.

She charged after her opponent as he ran again and hurled knives back at her without looking to aim. She flicked her fingers to knock them out of line one after the next, then fell into a slide again as a pot of boiling water arrowed at her face. Her shield probably would have handled it, but it was always better not to get hit in the first place.

Danica bounced back up and threw frost magic in front of him on the floor. He slid, which made her laugh since it was such petty revenge on her part since he'd done the same to her. He spun and waved his hands at her. She saw the wall of force shimmering as she hurtled toward it at a dead run. She reached out with her left hand, the other occupied by a pistol, and waved it in a tight circle.

Lightning shot out to create that same circle on the force wall. The bolts gathered in the center at first, then spread out. Her magic cut a hole in his, and she dove through as she reached it. It snapped tight on the force shield around her ankle, but her momentum carried her through, and she shoulder-rolled back up to her feet.

A glimmering portal stood in front of him. She growled, "Hell no," grabbed the lanyard on her backpack, and yanked it. A moment later, his escape route vanished as the anti-magic field enveloped it. He twisted, snarled, "Witch," then ran again.

She called, "I'm not a witch. Do you see a wand? How about you stop running?" He didn't reply, so she buckled down and pushed herself to run faster. There was no way he would get away from her.

CHAPTER THREE

anica was starting to breathe heavily as she pelted after him. She would have pushed magic into her muscles to help but couldn't give him the opportunity to portal again.

As she burst out a heavy steel door, evening twilight replaced the bright interior light. Chatter over her earpiece focused on goings-on inside the hotel with no comment on her pursuit. It made sense. She wasn't part of the team, only an observer. Now she was a free agent.

Her foe dashed across two lanes of traffic, and she deactivated the backpack long enough to slam force magic into the ground to fly over and gain some ground on him. He turned into an alley, and she followed, spotting him farther away than expected. The analytical part of her brain pointed out that magic could be used for speed, too, and she told it to shut up as she yanked the lanyard again. She fired a round at the wall and shouted, "Stop, or I'll shoot."

He stopped and turned with his hands raised as she slowed to a walk. His face was entirely ordinary, although it was notably more vertical than horizontal as if someone had squeezed him. It reminded her of cartoon villains.

His smile widened as he observed, "You're all alone."

The way he said it was warning enough. She threw herself to the side, into the cover of a metal dumpster next to the back door of a restaurant as bullets slammed into the bin.

Danica yanked the lanyard again and used a force blast to send her cover rolling down the alley at high speed. It slammed into her foe and knocked him down as she got to her feet and ran forward. She automatically noted where the bullets were coming from and saw her opponent's two protectors in the slight cover of doors in the alley's brick walls. She reached out with her magic to steal the gun of the one on the left and shot hers at the one on the right to drive him back into his minimal protection.

When her pistol clicked empty and he leaned out to shoot at her, she ripped his gun from his grip as she ran down the alley. Once she had the angle, she hit both men with force blasts, sending one back to smash his head against the metal door behind him and the other through the door into the room beyond. She yelled at the man she'd been chasing, who was some distance away. "Would you just stop, you bastard?" She halted her run and aimed the gun she'd stolen squarely at the man's back.

A van pulled up as the man threw himself to the ground. The driver leveled a rifle at her as the side door slid open and another man jumped out and sent a fireball flying at her. Danica retreated under the barrage of magic and metal. She got her first break of the day when the rifle wasn't loaded with anti-magic ammunition, but the barrage meant she couldn't kill magic with the backpack again. She threw a fireball down the line at her foe, who countered it with frost.

The resulting collision filled the alley with steam that obscured her vision, but she resisted the almost over-whelming urge to dash into it in pursuit. When it dissipated, the van was pulling away. She charged after it with magically enhanced speed, but it was already turning a corner onto the highway a block away.

She snarled a curse and growled, "Competent enemies be damned," then headed back into the alley. There, she discovered the two men she'd taken down were gone. She put her hands on her hips and shook her head as she shouted at the walls, "I mean *really* damned. Like, demons come up and rip your soul out of you kinda damned. Not just everyday ordinary kind of damned."

She pushed sweaty hair out of her face and jogged toward the hotel, realizing that having done the whole pursuit in pumps hadn't done her feet any favors. She reached the ballroom without further incident and discovered the guests being inspected one by one before they were allowed to leave the room.

Arthur Blackwood walked up to her. He was a little over six feet tall, trim, and athletic. His skin was appropriately pale for someone from England, and he had perfectly styled salt-and-pepper hair. All in all, he was quite handsome and reveled in that fact.

He asked, "Any luck?"

She shook her head, then removed the magazine from the pistol and racked the slide to remove the round. She handed the items to Arthur. "I doubt you'll get anything off this, but I took it from a bad guy. The one I borrowed from your people is in the alley outside."

He accepted it. "Just couldn't resist getting into the mix, could you?"

Danica laughed. "I'm not good at standing around watching when things are happening. Should I have cowered in the corner? Maybe rounded up the other fancy ladies for a chat session?"

He raised an amused eyebrow. "Somehow I can't see you hanging out with this crowd."

"Me neither. First, I doubt they'd have me, and second, you know, any group that will allow me in is probably not one I want to be part of."

Arthur laughed. "I've heard your father say that so many times."

She rolled her eyes. "Yeah. Apple doesn't fall far from the tree. I know. I've only heard it about seven thousand times so far."

"Well, he was an investigator, and you are an investigator. That's a choice you made."

"He was military. What I do is rather different."

Arthur nodded. "But no less challenging." He gestured at the trustees, who were visibly shaken and seated at a different table with guards around them. "What do you make of this?"

Danica gazed around the room with analytical eyes.

"I'm guessing they were in here early to avoid the scanners. Maybe they hid below the stage. Might be worth seeing if there's a crawlspace underneath."

"Already on that."

"I didn't sense the magical or the veil, but my ability is temperamental. Sometimes it works, other times it doesn't."

He nodded at someone across the room who had signaled a question. "Well, I'm glad it worked this time. You might have saved the lives of those trustees."

"I doubt it. They could've pulled the triggers from behind the veils if that's what they wanted. Are you thinking ransom?"

Arthur shrugged one shoulder. "Extortion of some kind. My guess would be company secrets or something rather than money, but you never know. There are easier targets to hit if you're looking for cash."

"I guess."

One of Arthur's people jogged up. "We have two captives, attackers who were knocked unconscious during the fight." He nodded at Danica. "You took down one of them. Nice job."

"I didn't fracture anything in his head, did I?"

"Not that our medic saw."

At least one thing had gone her way that night. "Good. I was surprised and let that punch get a little away from me."

The new arrival replied, "I'd say you did perfectly. People who try to attack by surprise don't deserve any regard from us."

Arthur asked, "Anything else to report?"

The man shook his head. "Only that they must've had a good retreat plan worked out in advance because no one can figure out how the other attackers got away. Probably another magical somewhere in the hotel."

Danica asked, "The anti-magic field wasn't everywhere?"

Arthur frowned. "No. That was our recommendation, but they didn't want to irritate any guests who might be using simple magics. So, they insisted only on portables."

She shrugged off the backpack and handed it to the guard. "Speaking of which, here you go."

He accepted it and looked at Arthur, who made a slight shooing motion. The man left, and Arthur queried, "So, what are your initial impressions of Spellbound Security?"

Danica shrugged. "That the company was smart to hire you all."

"We'd like to think so. Obviously, it's too soon for you to give me a full report. Why don't we do that tomorrow at breakfast?"

She looked around the room to see if she had anything else to offer, but his people had it all well in hand. "What would you like me to do now?"

He smiled. "Go up to your suite. Maybe nap a bit. Room service or the beach party, whatever makes you happy. I owe you even more now than I did at the start of this thing, so consider this an all-inclusive experience for you." He pointed a finger. "Not including shopping. The stores here are ridiculous."

Danica laughed. "I *did* have my eyes on one of the Gucci bags."

"My largesse does not extend that far."

She stuck out her tongue, then countered, "Okay, I'll clear out the hotel minibar while I dream of shopping."

Arthur winced. "Maybe consider the beach party instead."

Danica laughed. "Don't worry. I'm not fancy. The beach party is perfect. See you in the morning."

CHAPTER FOUR

The next morning, after thoroughly enjoying the beachfront party the night before and staying up too late because of it, Danica headed down for breakfast. She'd chosen a casual look of jeans and a decent top with comfortable boots.

As predicted, her feet ached from the efforts of the night before. She could have handled the pain with a few sips of a healing potion but figured it was better to endure it as a reminder not to wear stupid shoes when she might have to chase an evildoer. She snorted inwardly. *Evildoer. Evildoer wannabe, more like.*

Arthur was already seated at a table on the plant-filled outdoor patio of the dining room and rose as she joined him. He was dressed in another stylish suit, his only concession to casual attire the lack of a tie and a single undone button. A fruit tray arrived as she sat, and the server promised to return for a further order in a moment.

Danica spotted a basket of croissants on the table. She took one, ripped it in half, and applied herself to the small pot of blackberry jam next to it. She moaned at the delicious taste, then washed it down with the coffee that appeared a moment later. "Okay. Whatever I had to go through last night was worth it for this breakfast."

Arthur laughed as he spread butter on his croissant. "Glad to hear it. How was your evening?"

She shook her head with a grin. "There are some serious party animals hanging out at this place. I finally escaped to my room at one, and I had the sense they were just getting started on their second wind."

"So I've heard. I'm more of a holding down a seat at the bar with a glass of whiskey kind of person, myself."

"You're missing out."

He waved it off. "I've already had my party days. It's no loss to slow down a little and enjoy the scenery."

Danica snorted. "As if. You're every bit as vibrant as I remember. Although…" She shook her head. "Never mind."

Arthur gave her a mock glare. "You were going to mention the thinning hair. I know you were. Don't deny it."

She laughed. "But it's doing it in a good way. Widow's peaks look good on you."

"Maybe one day you'll come to understand the intense pain you have caused me." He took a sip of coffee and patted his lips with a napkin. "So, tell me your impressions of last night."

Danica speared a strawberry and chewed it as she put her thoughts into order. "The setup was good. Having the two undercover at the table was brilliant and was probably the only thing that allowed us to react quickly enough to mess up the attack. Your people were all loose but attentive, which is my preference for such an operation. The outer cordon seemed to fall apart a bit, though." Her voice went up at the end to indicate it was a question.

Arthur nodded. "It did. They were drawn away by some shouts and strange noises and received permission to go investigate."

She frowned. "I didn't hear that."

"You weren't on the command channel with the team lead. I didn't want him feeling like he was being watched."

Danica raised an eyebrow. "Even though he was."

Arthur nodded. "Even though he was."

"That's not very transparent of you."

He waved dismissively. "You Americans, with your equality and democracy and openness. I'm from England. We do things differently there."

She snorted. "Yeah, that whole royalty thing seems *really* useful."

He rolled his eyes. "I didn't say all of it was better." They laughed together, and he asked, "What else?"

She ordered eggs Benedict and accepted a coffee refill, then sipped it. "Your team's fighting skills were first-rate. I like that they didn't immediately go for their guns once I'd taken care of the attackers' weapons."

Arthur interrupted, "Good tactic, by the way. We'll add that to our standard repertoire whenever we have magicals on our team."

She nibbled on her croissant. "Probably not the smartest approach since it's akin to shooting someone in the leg when you could've shot them in the face, I suppose. I could've knocked them out with force blasts to the head, but that wasn't where my instincts took me."

Arthur nodded with a serious expression. "The first is the soldier's response. It's one I've had to break in myself more than once. It's not a bad thing that you prefer less immediately fatal options when you can." His voice turned sharper. "But only when you can. There will be moments that protecting your principal requires you to go the other way."

Danica returned a soft laugh. "Well, my position at Castle Investigations doesn't generally require me to handle protection."

"What did you think of our opponents' mix of forces?"

"Still think there were only two magicals inside, and the rest weren't?"

He nodded.

"If I'd been doing the attack, I would've wanted at least one more magical to handle surprises. Although they had one outside, so maybe that counts. Did you get anything useful from the two you captured?"

Arthur replied, "They've been turned over to the police and have asked for their lawyers. My sense is that they were freelancers, not the ones who decided to take a shot at the trustees. The magicals might've been part of the latter, or maybe just the one you chased was."

She nodded. Her thoughts had traveled in the same direction. "Do you think they're part of some group with an ax to grind?"

Arthur leaned back and sipped his coffee. "My instincts say yes. But they could be mercenaries, too. Magicals are in demand in that field."

Danica chuckled. "Maybe I should reconsider my line of work."

He set his cup down, leaned forward, and met her eyes. "Maybe you should."

A dozen thoughts tried to pass through her mind simultaneously, creating a traffic jam that left her speechless. After a few moments, she gulped some coffee to get her brain in order and wiped her mouth with a napkin. "Are we talking about the same thing here?"

Arthur laughed. "Probably not, given how unpredictable your brain is. I'd like to offer you a job."

"First, mean. Second, I have a job."

"At which you are underutilized. This would be a better job for someone of your prodigious talents."

Her eggs Benedict arrived, and she took a bite and chewed. He had selected an omelet and bit into a piece with obvious delight. She asked, "You've been checking up on me?"

"Of course. Your mother would have my head if I didn't."

Danica laughed. Her family lived across the country in California. She saw them fairly often since portals made some travel easy, but they had their own lives now, and so did she. "What have you reported back to them?"

"Just what I said. That you're excellent at your job but it's too small for you."

She nodded. There was some truth to the statement, and she'd been thinking about what her next step might be. "What are you planning, then?"

"I want to open another office. We plan to locate it in Cleveland as a favor to a friend, although it will have responsibility for much of the middle north of the country and DC. We don't have any clients in the capitol at the moment, but we might eventually. Competition is tough there."

"What would this branch do?"

He waved his fork, and a piece of his breakfast fell onto his dish. "Same as the others. Handle protection for those who need it. However they need it. It will involve a lot of travel since although you'll be based in Cleveland, where your principal goes, so do you."

Danica enjoyed traveling and liked a challenge. Things were lining up on the positive side of the spectrum. Then she realized something. "While I was watching your people, you were watching me, weren't you?"

He pointed a finger. "See? You're smart."

"Did you know there would be an attack?"

"No. I would never have endangered you, my people, or the trustees had I known. But I was able to watch how you worked and interacted with people, and it confirmed what I already knew. You're ready to lead a team rather than simply being a part of one, and your skill set is perfect for what my company does."

Danica frowned, uncomfortable with the compliments. "What kind of support will I have?"

Arthur paused to chew, swallow, and take a sip of coffee. "Whatever you need. Most of our locations have tech support, an infomancer, street-level people, and at least a second-in-command. If you need more and can justify why, you'll get more."

"All right, let's suppose I say yes. How does it work?"

"You give your two weeks' notice. After that, you head up to Cleveland. I'll lease a place for you to live for the first six months while you decide whether this is something you want to do long-term. If it is, you'll get a housing allowance. The company, of course, will pay you well."

She laughed. "Exorbitantly, I hope."

He shook his head. "*Well.* Neither of your parents would forgive me if I didn't make you earn your way."

"I know. That's the worst thing about them."

They laughed together again, then ate in silence for several moments until Arthur broke it. "So, want to join the team?"

Danica smiled. "No. I want to *lead* the team."

His expression stretched to match hers. "Perfect. Let's talk details."

CHAPTER FIVE

A couple of weeks later, after wrapping up her work at Castle Investigations, Danica flew to Cleveland. Arthur had provided a first-class ticket, which was a new experience for her, and she'd enjoyed the snacks and coffee drinks included in her morning flight.

Arthur met her at the airport and pointed out various landmarks and neighborhood names she struggled to keep straight in her mind as he drove her through the city. It always took her a while to get properly settled in a new place, and she was sure this would be no exception.

After taking a couple of bridges that spanned a modest river, he pulled into a small neighborhood of storefronts across the water from what looked like a huge industrial center. As they climbed out of the SUV, he remarked, "People seek us out, so there's no need to pay for high-rent real estate up on the Gold Coast or anything."

She chuckled. "Gold Coast?"

Arthur gestured. "The lake drives a lot of things around

here. It's really very pretty for three-quarters of the year. Winter, not so much."

Danica replied, "I like snow."

That caused him to laugh for several seconds. "Well, good, because there's a lot of the stuff around in the cold months."

"Not like Miami, then."

"This will be my first hazardous climate office. Unless you count storm flooding." He unlocked the front door of the two-story freestanding building and led her inside. The entrance opened onto a reception area with a big, curved desk a handful of steps inside. An inner wall separated the lobby from the back section, which was organized into a fairly standard layout of offices plus a small conference room. A kitchen area and restrooms made up the rest of the back section.

Danica looked at Arthur. "Pre-furnished?"

He nodded. "Yeah, this stuff is all from the people who had it last. We're leasing, so I didn't want to completely redecorate. I know it needs some work, and you can do whatever you like, within reason."

She laughed. "Gucci furniture?"

An exaggerated eye roll prefaced his response. "I don't think that's a thing, but if it is, no." He led her up a narrow flight of stairs to the building's second floor. That level was wide open and empty, nicely lit by the sunlight streaming through the plentiful windows on all sides. The floor was beat-up wooden planks, and the walls seemed to be the same brick as on the outside.

Danica asked, "Someone thought about renovating this space but stopped?"

"Exactly. They ripped out the old stuff but never managed to put in the new stuff. I figured it might be useful as a gym or small training area, depending on your preferences."

She looked it over with a critical eye as she walked around with the floor creaking under her with each step. "I love the floor, but it's not very practical if we'll be doing anything strenuous up here. Would probably be quite the racket downstairs."

He replied, "Whatever you need, you can do."

She said the last words in unison with him. "Within reason."

Arthur laughed. "All right, let me show you the best part." He walked down the stairs, opened a door she hadn't noticed, and led her down another flight. This one was narrower than the last.

The building's basement was set up as a storage space with mostly empty shelves and racks all around. A large barn door-style barricade stood at one end, and it rolled aside at the press of a button to reveal a tunnel and a half-dozen lime green scooters.

Danica asked, "Scooters?" They seemed so out of place.

Arthur nodded. "Scooters. You'll be able to portal, of course, but your team might not all be magicals." They climbed on the vehicles and he led the way down the concrete tunnel. Lights activated as they approached, doubtless tied to motion sensors, and extinguished as they passed.

She zoomed up beside him. "This is kind of creepy. Real serial killer vibe."

He laughed. "That's one way to describe it."

"What was this for?"

"According to what I was able to dig up, this tunnel goes back to the years of Prohibition. It was supposedly used to move illegal alcohol from place to place."

She curved the scooter to the left to avoid a puddle. "That's pretty bold and entrepreneurial."

"I couldn't agree more. I'm not sure how the economics of it worked out overall, but it's convenient for us."

They rolled to a stop before a similar barn door-style barricade with identical scooters parked outside. They set theirs into two of the charging stations built into the wall, then Arthur entered a code in the keypad beside the door. It slid aside, and she heard the sound of the movement echoing in the space beyond. They stepped through into a huge open structure that was multiple stories high.

Danica looked around in amazement. "What is this place?"

Arthur grinned. "I thought you'd like it. This is your functional base of operations, as opposed to the public-facing side at the other end of the tunnel."

"Okay, what was it before it became our base of operations?"

He gestured, and she followed him toward the center until she could see unobstructed. "This side was warehouse space. The big doors over there, the rails set into the concrete floor, that's all pretty obvious. Incoming and outgoing cargo, plus storage all over the rest of this part." He gestured toward massive pieces of equipment on the far side of the building, the gantries above, and several other things she couldn't immediately identify. "This other area was used as an assembly line. For train parts, I read. Wheels, maybe."

Danica shook her head. "Damn. This is really ours?"

"It is. I bought it for a song, and if the Cleveland office doesn't work out, I'll turn it into a rental storage space."

Danica turned in a circle, her gaze sweeping from the floor to the skylights high above on the pitched roof, then back down. It was an enormous amount of space. "We could do a lot with this."

Arthur looked pleased with himself. "I would expect nothing less from you. Now, if you'd be so kind, how about a portal back to the other building?"

Danica opened one, and they stepped through. Arthur walked to the back and made coffee while she prowled the place again. It was hard to believe it was hers. Technically, she didn't own it, but she would make it either a success or a failure. *No,* she corrected mentally. *She would make it a success.*

When she came back downstairs, Arthur was seated in the cramped conference room with a mug of coffee in hand. Another sat on the table next to him. She snagged it and headed for the kitchen, where she found some sugar in a cabinet, brought it back to the table, and dumped some into her mug.

He scowled. "How can you engage in such an abomination? Coffee should not be touched by anything other than coffee."

Danica sipped it and smiled. "That's your opinion. I like fancy coffees."

"There it is. The dark secret that would've prevented me from hiring you had I known it beforehand."

Danica laughed as she sat. "Your mistake. So, additional personnel seems to be the next step, right?"

Arthur nodded. "If you follow the model of the other branches, you'll need a techie and an infomancer as support staff, plus some people who can work in the field."

"That was my thought, too."

"You'll want to get a mix of looks and personalities. Not all your people should be obvious as guards, although you'll definitely want someone who can be a visible and obvious deterrent, as well."

Danica raised an eyebrow. "Are you saying I'm not that?"

A smile curved his lip. "People might tend to underestimate you."

She fluffed her blonde hair and adopted a vacuous expression. "Like, I guess." They laughed, and she asked, "Do you have recommendations?"

He gestured at her with his mug. "See, I knew you were smart. I do."

"Should we invite them here after we get the place cleaned up a little?"

Arthur shook his head. "No, I think it might be better if you got a look at them in their natural environments."

Danica sipped her coffee, then put more sugar in to poke him. "All right. You have three successful offices, so I guess you know a bit about this stuff."

He drawled, "You're so kind. I'll have my people set it up for the next few days."

"Perfect."

He stood, and she did the same as she asked, "What now?"

He fished in his pocket and tossed a set of keys to her. "First, you portal me back to Miami. Then, you go check out your place. I think you'll like it."

35

CHAPTER SIX

Danica climbed into the SUV and started the engine. Arthur had explained that it was leased to the company, which meant she could use it whenever she needed it until others joined her in the office. She dialed in her destination to the car's GPS, and a projection showing her path appeared on the windshield at the edge of her vision.

She followed the yellow line as she drove over the rivers, through downtown, and into suburbs and neighborhoods. They changed from closely packed buildings to less crowded ones until finally, she turned off a main road into a neighborhood of single-family homes. Her house was at the back, a small two-story structure with a driveway that led to a single-car garage.

Danica pulled into the driveway and climbed out of the SUV. The place was painted a deep shade of green that looked like it would need a fresh coat before too long. The roof shingles were a similar color, and the door and window frames were all freshly painted white. The front door was also white and opened to the keys on the ring.

Inside, a staircase to the left climbed to the second floor. To the right was a living room with a comfortable-looking couch that curved from one wall to the next. A wall-mounted TV was on the wall opposite it, and a coffee table in between looked like the perfect place to rest feet while watching.

The first floor lacked inner walls, so she could see the dining room and kitchen that were side-by-side in the space toward the back. She'd seen open-concept layouts before but had never lived in one. She imagined what it would be like to have friends over and be able to cook in the kitchen while chatting with everyone.

It was a little small for a permanent place, but Arthur had said the lease was for six months, the same as the lease on the office building. She had that long to get Spellbound Security's Cleveland office rolling and profitable, or pointed in that direction. It was a challenge she relished.

Danica had built many clubs, organizations, and small groups during her college days spent studying criminology and investigation. She had shown a knack for it and liked to think she also had a knack for leadership. She laughed and said out loud, "Well, I guess we'll figure out if that's true over the next six months or so."

Her boss at Castle Investigations had been sorry to see her leave but had understood when she explained why. He'd told her she could always come back, but he knew she wouldn't because she'd be a success at whatever she tried. She'd thanked him for the vote of confidence and again for offering her a backup plan in case she failed. Danica wasn't a stranger to failure, but what she tried worked out the way she wanted it to more often than not.

She checked the basement, which was unexpectedly small and home to a washer, dryer, and some storage. Back on the first floor, she took the door out into the garage. It was barely large enough to store a car, with a couple of shallow shelving units along the back wall.

Upstairs in the house were two small bedrooms and one large bathroom that had been recently redone. She wondered again who might've lived here and why they might have made that choice and sent a word of thanks out to the universe for them. The pristine bathtub was plenty large enough for her to soak in, and it had a separate fancy-tiled glassed-in shower. It was perfect.

She slid her suit jacket off, tossed it aside, and opened a portal to the apartment she was leaving behind. Her possessions were all boxed, and she grabbed the first one she could find that contained clothes. After changing into jeans and a T-shirt, she brought the rest of her belongings from the old place to the new with a combination of magic and muscle. The flight and riding around afterward had left her feeling stiff, and carrying the boxes up and down the stairs did a good job of warming up her muscles and stretching them out.

She had moved all of them by the time dusk came around. A nearby restaurant delivered pizza and a twelve-pack of cold soda. When it arrived, she relaxed and ate a few slices while wandering around outside the house. The most impressive sight was the forest that bounded the property's backyard. The front yard was also nice, but trees always spoke to the elven part of her heritage.

The backyard had only grass and a few bushes, which seemed appropriate with the thick trees beyond. She found a lawn chair in the garage and brought it out, then sat and drank Coke as the sun disappeared and the moon began its climb. Once the sun was completely out of view, Danica sat cross-legged in the grass and steepled her fingers before her chest. She envisioned the magic within her as a body of water deep in the center of her body, then imagined it flowing up through her torso, down her arms, and into her hands. She turned her palms toward the forest and let her power flow outward.

She felt a connection with the Earth first and sensed the life within it. The trees were a powerful presence as they relaxed into the quiet of evening, turning mostly dormant until the next day's sunshine inspired them again. She felt the currents in the Cuyahoga River as it moved through Cleveland and the massive, almost overwhelming power of the lake some distance away.

She had never lived this close to such a large body of water, although she'd visited oceans on vacation. To sense that she was now part of this particular life system was daunting. She breathed it all in, let it flow into her, and breathed it out again, imagining the power continuing down into the earth.

A strange flavor made itself known on the edge of her tongue, something on the line between tart and bitter that triggered thoughts of power and magic in her. It didn't register as a threat, so she opened herself to it rather than shutting down the connection. The tugging at her senses drew her to her feet and enticed her to walk toward the tree line. A simple word and gesture summoned a ball of lightning into her hand that illuminated the area around her.

An opening she hadn't noticed gave her entry into the forest. No obvious trail lay inside, and she moved with caution as she slipped between the trees to avoid twisting an ankle. She'd come out barefoot to feel the connection to the ground and had wrapped her feet in force magic before entering the forest, but that wouldn't protect the joint if she did something dumb.

As she moved deeper into the thick greenery, the pull of power led her on a diagonal toward her right that carried her deeper into the woods. The flickers of life around her were impossible to ignore, insects and small animals moving about in their nightly rituals. All she sensed from the area ahead of her was a strange emptiness. Finally, she arrived at a small clearing dominated by two tall trees in the center that had grown up side-by-side and were connected by a branch that had grown from one and grafted into the other to create a type of arch.

Stones that were placed too symmetrically to be random created a boundary in a half-circle around the trees. She sent a questing tendril of magic toward them and felt the wards placed on the stones. They were a warning of danger that would probably cause a human to turn away, but not a barrier to prohibit access.

She circled and found the same arrangement on the opposite side. Nothing about it seemed dangerous, but she was positive the area hid something. Her magic pushed her to go through the arch. She asked the trees, "Well, aren't you interesting?"

The normal sounds of the woods were the only reply.

Danica cloaked herself in multiple layers of force shields tucked tight against her skin, steeled herself against whatever surprise might await, and stepped across the stone barrier. When she did, the sight before her changed.

The gap between the trees was no longer empty but filled with a portal that led to another piece of forest. She didn't know where that might be or if it was on Earth. It could be a portal to the magical planet Oriceran, from which all the magic on this planet had originated. Danica shrugged inwardly. Wondering about it wouldn't accomplish anything, and she still didn't sense any specific danger. She walked through the portal.

CHAPTER SEVEN

The other side of the portal deposited her onto a trail that struck her as lightly traveled but well-kept. Tall trees rose on both sides, their branches arching over to intertwine with one another high above, but no leaves lay on the walkway. The space between them was narrow, the trees just beyond her fingertips when she stretched her arms. It felt as if giants on both sides were watching her.

Danica walked forward slowly and let her magical senses spread out in every direction. From the other side of the portal, this place had seemed innocuous. Now, it felt distinctly oppressive with an edge of threat.

A peculiar power she sensed with taste and smell suffused the space as if it was woven into every tree and fallen leaf that bordered the path and into the dirt. She'd never been in a place that offered such a uniform feeling. Normally, the currents of magic brought different flavors to her senses. Here, it was one flat sensation.

No, not flat, she corrected herself as she walked. It had an edge, like a sheet of glass with some pieces sticking up here and there as traps for the unwary. A silent effort of will expanded her ball of light to keep a better eye out for trouble. Her senses cued her to the fact that the trail was ending, although what was ahead looked the same. She paused before realizing it was probably another illusion like the one that had hidden the portal.

Stepping through it revealed an oval-shaped clearing lit by a silvery glow that could have been moonlight had there been a moon above rather than only stars. She stood at one point, and a strangely organic-looking house occupied the other. It seemed to have been grown from tree branches or maybe roots.

She muttered the words that would allow her to see through illusions, but it remained unchanged. This meant it either looked like that, or she couldn't counteract the magic of the place.

In front of the house sat a large ornate rocking chair that had also been grown rather than constructed. It held a woman with an unsettling smile. At first, Danica thought she was old because of the long white hair that trailed down over her shoulders and into her lap. A closer look at the woman's face showed only pale, unwrinkled skin and bright, intelligent eyes. Black makeup adorned the area around her eyes and lips. The woman said in an amused tone, "Welcome. It's been some time since anyone crossed that portal to visit me."

Danica offered a respectful nod and a slight bow. "I appreciate the welcome. I'm Danica Grey."

The woman laughed, and it rang like crystal wind chimes in the space. "So forward, giving me your names. They have the ring of truth to them. And not one, but two of them." She shook her head. "Dangerous things, names."

Danica shrugged. "Perhaps to the superstitious."

"Oh, you believe you know all there is to know about magic, then?"

"I would never claim that. But I know a bit." A slight scratching at the edge of her mind caused her to reinforce her mental barriers, and she threaded energy ever so gently into her muscles and senses. Something seemed wrong here, and she needed to be ready for whatever might come.

The woman waved a hand. It, too, was young-looking, with shining black fingernails that extended an inch beyond the tips. "Well, now. Can I offer you some tea?"

Danica smiled. "I know better than to accept tea from strangers, especially those who mention the power of names."

"Oh, now you think I might be fae. How cute. No, I am as human as you." She tilted her head to the side. "Which is to say, not wholly human."

"But there is a trace, at least?"

The woman made another negligent gesture with her hand. "A tiny drop, back somewhere in the bloodlines."

"So, what do you do here?"

"Live. Laugh. Love." Her laughter burst out of her again. "Did I get it right? Is that the trite saying?"

"It is." Danica wondered where she had heard or seen it. Maybe the woman came out of her clearing now and again to interact with the normal world. *She'd fit right in around Halloween, that's for sure.*

The woman's mood changed, trading levity for gravity.

"Unfortunately, it's not acceptable for people to trespass into this place. Even those who aren't entirely human."

"I apologize if I offended. How can I make it right?"

The woman leaned back in her chair with a satisfied smile. "By feeding my pets."

A soft, melodic voice came on the breeze and whispered in Danica's ear. "Beware the trees."

She slapped an additional shield around herself as the trunks and branches of nearby trees came alive and reached for her. They stopped at her shields, but the inward pressure was strong enough that eventually, they would buckle.

Her first thought was to portal away before they gave in, but her instinct said doing so would be potentially stepping into a trap. The other woman had allowed her this space, this delay to react. She might have a way to redirect a portal into somewhere awful, like deep into the earth or the World In Between. No, she needed to fight her way free and get out the way she came in, or at least get clear of the woman's presence before she portaled.

As her shield constricted further, Danica focused her power into her hands. Cylinders of force grew in them, then a scimitar-shaped blade made of fire extended from the cylinders. The martial arts she'd studied all had one useful thing in common. The techniques were equally useful with fists or weapons. She let the outer shield fall and sprang into action as the trees reached eagerly for her.

Her flaming scimitars hacked and slashed at the encroaching limbs. They were quick, but she pumped more magic into her muscles and reflexes to be faster. She ignored the twigs that scratched at her shields but cut off anything branch-sized or larger as it encountered her defenses. She backpedaled steadily, carefully placing one foot behind the next and testing for purchase before committing her weight. A rock under her foot that sent her to the ground might be the end of her.

The voice whispered again. "Below."

Danica reinforced the portions of the shields positioned under her feet as roots erupted from the ground. They twined around her shields in an effort to tie up her legs. She created a flaming shield between her outermost force shield and the next one in, then dispelled the former. The roots retreated, writhing and waving as they grabbed only flames. The branches did the same higher up, giving her a moment to breathe and smile at her success.

A blast of cold magic hit her without warning, and her gaze snapped up. The woman was on her feet with one arm outstretched. The attack had dispelled her fire shield, but not the ones beneath it. She continued to hack and slash at the roots and branches with her flaming swords.

The other woman smiled as if she was enjoying the sight of Danica's flailing. She considered throwing attacks directly at the woman, then considered it again because she *really* wanted to do it. But she had trespassed, and while this seemed like an overreaction by the other woman, it was always possible she was in the wrong.

Moments later, she was on the trail again. The illusion in front of her had made the clearing disappear. She stopped to bolster her shields and kept her swords up. The voice commented, slightly louder than before, "You have escaped her, for now. I don't think she'll pursue."

Danica looked around but didn't see anything. "Who are you?"

A glimmer in the air before her resolved into a small creature flying at shoulder height. It was a beautiful dragon in miniature. Its tiny scales were primarily purple with accents of orange, yellow, and a couple splashes of red. The butterfly-shaped wings were the only departure from the look of a standard dragon. Danica had never seen such a creature before but was awestruck by it. Its mouth stretched into a smile as if noting her appreciation with pleasure. It flapped a few times, then landed on her force-covered shoulder. She felt its talons dig into the magic to hold on as she introduced herself. "I'm Danica."

The creature uttered a high-pitched laugh. "I know. I heard. I am Jilalavarie. I know that's a mouthful. You can call me Jilly since you're my human now."

CHAPTER EIGHT

Danica's mind whirled as she walked back toward her house. The little dragon was still on her shoulder as she left the forest and stepped onto her lawn. She kept going into the house and headed into the kitchen. The dragon jumped off her shoulder, flapped her iridescent wings, and neatly landed on the counter. Danica realized her magical senses had tracked the creature's movements, which meant she was already connected to the tiny dragon without having made any effort to do so. She hit the buttons to make coffee, then turned to her guest. "Would you like some tea with honey?"

The little dragon hopped up once on the counter in reply. "Of course. I love honey."

Danica looked through the box of kitchen items she hadn't yet unpacked and found two different containers of tea. "Jasmine or chamomile?"

"Both."

Danica laughed at the dragon's earnest answer. "All right, then." She heated water in a kettle, then poured it into a cup with two teabags. When it was ready, she took out the honey. "Say when."

She poured for several seconds before Jilly chirped, "When."

Danica carried the cup to the table and sat in one of the chairs. The dragon flew over and landed next to the cup. Danica warned, "Careful, hot."

The dragon blew on it, which made Danica laugh. When she laughed, Jilly did as well. The dragon said, "I can feel your feelings. In here." She tapped her chest with a wingtip.

Danica replied, "I can sense you with my magic, too."

"You're an elf." It was a statement, not a question.

"Part elf, part human."

"Even a part elf is an elf, just like a part dragon is a dragon."

Danica tilted her head. "So that's what you are? A dragon?"

"Of course. Can't you tell?"

"To be honest, I didn't know if dragons existed before this moment. I've never seen one. And especially not one your size. No offense."

Jilly laughed. "It's good to be tiny."

Danica sipped her coffee. "How did you wind up in there?"

The dragon sipped from her cup as if echoing Danica's actions. Her demeanor changed to something more serious, and the playful expression left her face, replaced by a more focused one. "I followed someone in. Foolish of me."

"From here?"

Jilly shook her head. "From another part of the forest. I

had seen people go in before and was curious about what they were doing. Curiosity can be a bad thing."

Danica nodded. "Sometimes. Was the woman in the clearing mean to you?"

"No. I hid from her. If she knew I was there, she never said so."

"What happened to the person you followed? Did the woman in the clearing kill her?"

Jilly took another long drink of tea. "No. The witch I followed asked some questions and left. I stayed behind, then discovered I couldn't make the portal appear by myself. It requires a different kind of magic than mine, I guess."

"What do you know about the woman?"

"I heard people talking about her. She's not evil, just solitary. While I was there, she spent a lot of her time reading. Some of her time was occupied with other visitors. I never felt comfortable following them out, though. They didn't seem like they'd come from here."

"Do you mean they came from Oriceran?"

The dragon replied, "From somewhere else. I only know this area."

"And then?"

"Then you came. The trees and roots were a test of skill and strength, I think. She's used them before. No one has ever been harmed."

Danica frowned. "That's not very neighborly."

Jilly laughed. "Fair."

"So why did you decide to leave with me?"

"It wasn't a place that felt good to me."

Danica nodded. "I had a similar reaction. Finish your

tea and honey and we'll see what we can do about making this a place that *does* feel good."

Danica took her mug with her to the couch. She'd deposited a box of important items in the living room while transferring things from her other place. Now she carefully lifted out the items she would need to cast wards of protection around the house. She'd had them in place at her previous apartment building, but they would need to be bound to this new place.

Each small figurine represented an animal of some kind. They'd been handed down from others in her family over the years and had originally been prizes in tea boxes. Each well-crafted miniature was about the size of her thumb. Her menagerie included different varieties of cats, dogs, rabbits, fish, whales, otters, and many more seemingly random animals.

Those who had taught her magic had always agreed that seven times seven was the correct number for warding. Thus she had forty-nine of them already imbued with some magic and about that many in reserve should something go awry with any of these. She occasionally traveled to flea markets or swap meets and bought the little figurines whenever she found them to add to her collection.

Also inside the box lay the ceramic bowl she used for ritual work, which had been repeatedly purified and imbued with the essence of her magic over the years. She placed the forty-nine statues into it and headed back into the kitchen.

Jilly leapt into the air and flapped her tiny wings to land on Danica's shoulder. Her claws sank into Danica's shirt but not into the flesh beneath, which she appreciated.

The dragon asked, "What are those?"

"Ward stones, of a sort."

"Any dragons?"

Danica laughed. "No, just ordinary creatures, not extraordinary ones."

Jilly laughed. "You said I was extraordinary. I'll remind you of that when you get annoyed with me."

"What makes you think I'll get annoyed with you?"

"Everybody does. It's part of my charm."

Danica laughed again. It seemed like it would be impossible to be unhappy with the tiny dragon around. "Well, all right then." She walked into the backyard, sat cross-legged on the ground, and placed the bowl in her lap. She closed her eyes and sent her senses spiraling outward. It was at first difficult to dampen the influence of Jilly's presence, which seemed to shine more powerfully than such a small creature should. After a couple of minutes, she managed to flow her magic around the dragon without any issue.

The power penetrated the ground in search of the next element she needed. She found a small open space filled with water and used force magic to open the earth around it. More force magic lifted the water and created a frame about it as it arced out of the ground to splash into the bowl and cover the statues. Jilly asked, "What's that for?"

"Purification and attunement to this place." Danica dipped one finger into the bowl and let her magic flow into the water. The liquid was already mostly pure, although it contained dirt and stone fragments. She swirled her finger, and everything that wasn't water came up to the top. A flick of that finger sent the debris flying out into the yard, leaving only what she needed behind.

Danica put both hands into the bowl and rubbed them over the statues, several at a time. She had to remove the influence of her previous place before she could attune them. She bent to the task while doing her best to leave any untainted traces of magic still in the statuettes undisturbed. It took several minutes.

Jilly walked from one shoulder to the other during that time, crossing the back of her neck. Danica had instinctively expected the claws to hurt on her skin, but they hadn't, and she wondered if that was part of the dragon's magic.

When the statues were clean, she took a handful out and left the rest inside as she set the bowl on the ground. She walked to the boundary of her property, which was marked by a fence that stretched from backyard to front on two sides, and set the first statue in place. It was a small owl.

Jilly asked, "Is that all there is to it?"

Danica shook her head. "No. We've connected it to this place, but not to me. That's what will truly make the wards work. Whenever I am here, I'll leach a small bit of power into them, and they will strengthen over time. But the only way I can do that is if I create a connection with them in this place, like the one I gave them with the land."

"Blood."

Danica nodded. "Always the best connector."

"Finger?"

Danica held up her thumb. The dragon's head snapped

forward, and Danica felt a brief pinch as the sharp teeth cut her skin. A drop of blood welled up. "Thank you."

Jilly laughed. "Always happy to help with whatever. Especially if it involves biting."

Danica chanted as she knelt and touched the statue with the drop of blood. The red vanished as it was sucked into the essence of the statue. She repeated the process with the others she placed along the boundary, then returned to the bowl for more. It took almost an hour to get them all arranged and attuned.

Once it was done, Danica smiled at the dragon on her shoulder. "Watch this."

She reached into the reservoir of magic at her core and pulled power up and out into her spread fingers. Twists of light emerged from them and moved around as if caught by a random breeze, twisting and twirling. Then, as if they were being drawn in, they spread out to flow into the statuettes, briefly making each one glow before the light show was sucked away. After a minute, she released the flow and smiled. She reached up and scratched the dragon on the unexpectedly tough scales under her chin. "How does it feel now?"

Jilly tipped her head to the side as if considering the question. "Safe."

"Good. Let's get some sleep. It's been quite a night."

CHAPTER NINE

The next day, Danica woke up early, showered, and dressed in what she considered her new professional look. The outfit consisted of a light-colored suit, a casual blouse underneath, and low-heeled boots since she'd learned her lesson in Tampa. A thin belt served no purpose other than style. Normally, she might've added her pistol and holster, but it wouldn't be necessary for today's outing. Besides, she always had her magic to turn to if trouble reared its ugly head.

Lacking any better idea of what to do with Jilly for the day while she was gone, she tapped her shoulder, and the dragon jumped on. Together, they walked through a portal from her neighborhood in Cleveland to the Spellbound Security offices in Miami. The receptionist looked up. He was a thin man with a broad smile and impressively long brown hair. She thought it made him look like a musician.

He remarked, "Mr. Blackwood is waiting for you." His gaze swept over to Jilly, but he said nothing about her.

Danica nodded. "I know the way, thanks." Arthur's door was open, and she breezed inside. He looked up with a smile, which broadened as he took her in. "I don't mean to alarm you, but you seem to have something on your shoulder."

Jilly flapped her wings as Danica laughed. "Yes, well, this is Spellbound Security Cleveland's first new employee. Jilalavarie, this is Arthur Blackwood. Arthur, this is Jilalavarie."

The dragon added, "Please call me Jilly."

Arthur replied, "A pleasure to meet you, Jilly." He shook his head and shifted his gaze to Danica. "Already causing trouble, are you?"

She laughed. "You knew what you were getting into when you hired me."

He rose and grabbed a set of keys from the corner of his desk. "It's true, I did. So, before we go to meet your new potential tech person, we have a small detour to make."

"What's that?"

"You'll see." They left the office and hopped into an SUV. He drove through the suburban streets around Miami with the knowledge of a local before pulling up at a restaurant that proclaimed itself a diner. A crowd stood outside.

She asked, "Breakfast, then? Feeling peckish?"

He chuckled. "No. Well, I am hungry, but that's another issue. The crowd isn't for the diner. It's for who's inside."

Danica noticed that some crowd members held signs, although she couldn't see what was written on them from behind and across the street. "What's the deal?"

"Shay Sands is a romance author. Some spicy stuff, apparently, and quite popular. She has a book signing two blocks away in a half-hour. Unfortunately, and against the wishes of her security, she decided to stop for breakfast. It seems like someone must've been watching her because this protest-slash-celebration showed up out of nowhere."

"Is she a client?"

Arthur shook his head. "No, but I know the leader of her team from way back. He asked for an extra set of eyes on short notice." He reached into the center console and pulled out a pair of glasses and an earpiece. "You're here, so that's you."

Danica laughed. "Awesome." She stepped out of the car and left the door open as she slipped off her jacket to better blend in with the crowd. She nestled the earpiece into place, donned the glasses, and told Jilly to wait in the car. She closed the door, wandered across the street, and moved to the side of the crowd to take a casual look at them.

Included were a mix of ages and races, both men and women. Some supported the author. Others were against her, with signs like Censor Shay and Shay Go Home.

She wondered if they'd been at the bookstore and run down here or if Arthur was right and someone had been spying on the woman. The crowd was shoving a little and yelling at the window that separated the restaurant's interior from the street. She didn't see the author from her perspective but had a bad angle on the interior.

A male voice sounded in her ear, youngish but professional. "Stand by for data."

A virtual overlay window opened on the right side of her glasses to provide a view from overhead. The way the image shook now and again confirmed it was a drone above her location. Another window opened to show the restaurant's interior.

She asked, "You hacked their security cameras?"

"You betcha. I'm no infomancer or anything, but they weren't particularly concerned about security, either." A third window opened beside the first two, which were stacked in the far right of her vision, to show a map view of the area.

"Can you move the map over to the left?"

It immediately snapped to the other end of her visual field. "Of course. I'm Zack, by the way."

"Danica. What else do you have for me?"

"How about the faces of some known problems for Shay Sands?"

"Perfect." The images flicked by one after the next. Again, they were a mix of male and female, and most had been taken from surveillance cameras. "Where did this come from?"

Zack replied, "Some are from security cameras at events, but most are from social media. People like to rant about her, both for and against."

Danica watched the parade of faces flick by. "What has them all riled up?"

"Couldn't tell you. I'm a thriller reader, myself."

Her gaze swept the crowd in an effort to match up pictures to faces. She glanced back at the car, saw Jilly watching her from a perch on the dashboard, and smiled at the dragon. She received one in return, then continued turning to look down the sidewalk. A face jogged her memory. "Do you see who I'm looking at?"

Zack replied, "Yeah, running facial recognition. Hold on." A few seconds later, one of the images she'd seen popped up. "His file reads as a low-level stalker. Probably not dangerous, but one of the folks her security keeps an eye out for."

"Are you in touch with them?"

"I can be."

She flicked her fingers and used magic to enhance her senses. "Warn them that he's here and tell them I'm going to intercept."

"Got it."

Danica adopted an innocuous smile as she ambled toward the man. His clothes looked thin, like he'd had them for a long time and they were barely holding on. His gaze stayed mainly on the ground as he walked in a strange, stuttering cadence. She thought he might be talking to himself, then noted that people might think she was. She raised a hand to cover her mouth. "You have any radio signals from him?"

Zack answered, "The drone's not outfitted to search for them, sorry."

"Okay." She kept walking toward him, and he took a step away to avoid a collision. At the same moment, she moved in the same direction. They bumped into each other, and her left hand snuck up under his jacket while her right reached down to his back pocket.

She muttered an apology and continued to frisk him. Her search came up with a switchblade. She pulled it out of his back pocket and held it up. He stammered something, and she shook her head. "Don't care. This is mine now. Turn around and go back the way you came if you don't want to get broken."

His gaze locked on hers, and he considered taking a shot at her. She let her smile widen a notch, and he deflated, turned, and walked away. She muttered, "One crisis averted," as she turned back toward the group.

Zack replied, "But another one pending. Shay is moving." In the little box that showed the camera inside the restaurant, she saw the author, another pair of people who looked like assistants or publicists, and several security guards rise from a table. They moved toward the front door.

She growled, "Why the hell aren't they going toward the back?"

"Don't know. I'm guessing security wanted to and was denied."

"I hope so, or she needs better security."

The door opened, and Shay's guards came out. The crowd immediately surged forward, but the men in the dark suits pushed back to clear space for the author. They moved with her as she walked along the window. Shay waved to her supporters and blew kisses to those shouting negative things at her.

Danica shook her head. "It's like she wants trouble."

"What is it they say? Any publicity is good publicity?"

"Those people are idiots."

Zack laughed. "Agreed. Better get a move on if you want to keep close."

She jogged toward the crowd. "See any problems?"

"Yeah. Look at the drone feed." Another crowd had

come from somewhere and was moving toward the author, her security, and the existing crowd from the direction of the bookstore. Danica muttered, "Dammit."

Zack said, "That about sums it up."

"Warn her security. I'm moving in close."

CHAPTER TEN

Danica pushed into and through the crowd until she reached the author's security team, using quick bumps of force magic to help clear her path of those who didn't take the hint. It required finesse to do it without injuring anyone, but she'd spent most of her life developing her abilities with magic. She had found many interesting and useful ways to employ her power.

The second crowd arrived and merged with the first, surprisingly with minimal conflict. Danica had expected the author's team to push through the second group, but instead they angled down an alley.

Zack muttered, "Uh-oh."

She snorted. "Yeah, uh-oh for sure. What kind of sensors do you have on that thing?"

"The usual. Visual. Sound. Thermal."

"Take a look at the cars on the next street. Do any have an unexpected number of people in them?"

The drone feed display in her glasses changed to show the thermal view of the cars on the street opposite the one they parked on. The image zoomed out, and she spotted a van that seemed to be packed with people as Zack commented, "That might be something."

She watched the author and her companions move down the alley toward that street. "It might. Do you have any weapons on that thing?"

"No. It's only a surveillance module."

"Okay." Danica was left more or less alone in the front of the restaurant as the crowd pushed into the alley behind the author. She looked up, assessed the distance, and blasted force magic into the ground to propel her up to the roof of the two-story building. After a clean landing, she turned, extended more force magic, and used it as a finger to tap Jilly.

The dragon looked up at her, and Danica gestured. A moment later, with the flapping of wings, the dragon landed on her outstretched palm.

Danica requested, "I'd like you to go down and look into the windows of a van on the next street." She jogged across the rooftop until she could look down at the street in question and pointed at the vehicle. It was still a decent distance away and maintained a steady pace. "That one. If you see any weapons, fly straight up. That will let me know you saw them."

The dragon laughed, then spoke in her mind. *Or I could just tell you.*

Danica blinked and replied, "Or you could just tell me."

Jilly laughed. "My human is silly." She flew toward the van.

Danica shook her head and muttered, "My life is so weird." She looked down into the alley. The guards had reorganized themselves so only one was leading Shay while the other four trailed to keep the crowd away from her. It made sense if the crowd was the imminent danger. Danica didn't think it was the threat, or not the only one. She wrapped force magic around herself in protective shields layered outward from her skin and wished she had brought a big gun.

Arthur spoke in her ear. "Anything?"

She replied, "Jilly's almost at the van. Stand by."

She watched the dragon circle the van, flying past the windshield and around to look in the other windows. A faint haze was visible around Jilly, and Danica wondered if her companion had built-in camouflage magic. Jilly sent, *They're holding things in their hands and wearing masks.*

Danica echoed the words, and Arthur replied, "That's good enough for me."

She replied, "Me too. Zack, have Shay's security get her moving to safety, no stops."

"On it."

Danica calculated the angles, then leapt down from the building. She used a burst of force magic at the bottom to cushion her fall. As soon as her feet were on the ground, she thrust her arms forward like a basketball player making a chest pass. A burst of force shot out of her palms, slammed into a car parked nearby, and hurled it into the path of the oncoming van. The two vehicles collided with grinding metal. To her left, crowd members behind Shay screamed, and the woman and her security ran down the street.

Danica shouted, "Jilly, keep an eye on Shay."

The dragon replied, *Of course,* and flew off after them.

She'd have to converse with her new companion about what offensive skills she possessed but was sure that whatever the dragon had, she'd use them to defend Shay. Danica focused her attention on the van. The engine was cranking, trying to start again, but she'd successfully broken something under the hood. She heard doors slide open on the opposite side, which told her they knew where the attack had come from and were using the van's body as protection.

Danica reached out with her force magic and wrenched the door off the car she'd used as a cue ball to take down the van. She threw a force shield in front of it and held it before her. Rifle fire sounded, but none of it hit the door, which meant they weren't using anti-magic rounds and thus weren't a threat to her. With a grin, she let her improvised shield fall, ran at the van, jumped onto the back of the car she'd used, and leapt into a kick.

Her brand of martial arts was a blend of several styles she'd studied and included the things she'd found most valuable from each. She had a variety of belts, none of which mattered to her as much as the skills she'd gained.

She pulled her leg back as she flew through the air and lashed out at the nearest enemy's chest as she came down. He brought his rifle up in an awkward block. She knocked the weapon into his chest and him backward into the back corner of the van. He crumpled as his head hit the metal.

Danica landed and put her back against the van. They were still shooting, not fully comprehending that their bullets weren't reaching her. She asked, "How many?"

Zack replied, "Four more, all on the opposite side."

She laughed to herself. "They must not have a lot of

experience at fighting magicals." She turned, reached deep for her magic, let it build for several seconds, and put her hands against the side of the van. Then she released the power through her palms. The van lurched away from her and slammed into the people hiding behind it. She'd only given enough force to knock it a couple of feet, not wanting to drop it on them, but it was enough to generate the sounds of curses, screams, and guns clattering on the ground.

Danica jumped to the van's roof and looked down. Two of her opponents were on the ground, seemingly unconscious. One had reached his feet, and another was struggling up. She pointed at the one who was fully upright and released a thread of lightning. The magical energy surrounded him and acted as a Taser would, surging through his nervous system and dropping him to the ground, unconscious.

That left one remaining, who made it upright as she jumped down to stand beside him. He twitched his rifle as if to bring it up from his side, and she slammed a burst of force magic into it that knocked it away. She demanded, "Who are you, and what's your intent?"

He shook his head, and his words were slightly slurred as he replied, "You're not the police. I don't need to talk to you."

She shrugged. "True. I can wait for my answers." She extended a hand and blasted him with lightning until he collapsed next to his friends. She opened the van's door and looked inside. They had brought a roll of duct tape, presumably for the author. She used it to bind their wrists behind their backs and their ankles, then to wrap them up in a group of four. Unless they were amazingly coordinated, they wouldn't be going anywhere.

Jilly sent, *Shay is safe in the bookstore.*

Danica echoed that information over the channel, and Arthur replied, "Good. Come on back. The police are on their way."

Zack added, "They're two minutes out."

She jogged to the bookstore to retrieve the dragon. Everything there looked completely under control. When she returned to the car, Danica looked at her employer. "If I didn't know you as well as I do, I'd say you'd put this together on purpose."

He laughed. "No, but I'm certainly not one to turn down an opportunity. I'm sure you guessed this by now, but Zack is the tech I'm recommending."

She smiled. "I figured that out, although not right away. You really are one to take advantage of the situation, Arthur."

He grinned. "Guilty as charged."

Danica asked, "So, Zack, feel like moving to Cleveland?"

"I already have my bags packed."

"All right then. Consider yourself hired."

CHAPTER ELEVEN

Zack was true to his word, and an hour and a half later, she met him in person at Arthur's office in Miami. He was lean but not skinny with bright hazel eyes, dark brown hair with an unexpected blue streak on one side, and an easy, somewhat awkward smile. He looked comfortable in his khakis and polo shirt, and ten silver rings glittered on his fingers. She figured he'd probably broken a lot of nerdy girls' hearts in the past.

He took her in at a glance. "Elf, huh?"

"Yeah, but how did you know? Is it Jilly?"

He laughed and extended a finger to the dragon. Jilly stuck her head out and allowed him to stroke a finger across the top of her head. "Those are some surprisingly hard scales."

The dragon replied, "I'm tougher than I look."

"I don't doubt it for a second. Fire breath?"

"Among other things."

Danica gently poked Zack. "Elf?"

"Oh. Your ears. The tops have the tiniest point, and

you don't seem like the kind to go in for aesthetic surgery. Which is the only way I've seen that on a non-elf."

She frowned. "People do surgery to have pointed ears?"

He nodded, seeming enthusiastic about the subject. "Lots of them, where I went to school. High school and college both. Most people consider it quite attractive." He realized what he'd said and added, "I didn't mean it that way."

Arthur commented, "Hitting on your boss on the first day is bad form."

Danica and Zack both laughed. The tech replied, "No, I'm never this smooth when I'm romantically involved with someone, trust me."

Danica considered teasing him but decided it would be inappropriate. She didn't know him well enough yet to cross that line just for a joke. "Good to know. Ready to see the new place?"

"You know it."

She opened a portal into the Cleveland office and waved him through. Behind his back, she met Arthur's eyes and rolled hers.

He laughed. "You're going to be great together, I can tell."

Jilly sent, *I like him.*

When she closed the portal, Zack stood in the doorway between the lobby and the office area behind it.

He commented, "Kinda small."

She showed him the upstairs, which he thought had potential, then took them to the basement and opened the security door to the tunnel.

"Scooters, awesome." He climbed on one and started rolling like he did it every day.

She caught up on hers. "So, scooter fan?"

"In my neighborhood—well, my old neighborhood, I guess—this is how I get around. Speaking of which, you'll portal me back, right?"

Danica laughed. "Yes, I'll be your magical transport until you get moved up here."

He grinned. "Perfect." They parked their scooters at the other end of the tunnel, and Danica entered the code and led him through the door. He turned in slow circles as he walked into the space. "Now this, *this* is what I'm talking about."

"It is pretty nice, isn't it?"

"Nice, hell. It's a dream come true. Assuming we have the funding to do something with it." He looked at her. "Do we have the funding to do something with it?"

Danica rolled her neck, which was a little stiff from her earlier exertions. She'd been off her normal exercise routine since taking the job and needed to fix that in short order. "Arthur says within reason but never explains what qualifies as 'within reason' for him. I'd say we figure out what we want to do and run it by him. If we have to cut, we'll cut, but better to ask for everything right off the bat, don't you think?"

Zack nodded. "Exactly how I'd want to do it. It looks like half this place is filled with an assembly line and the other half is open for our use, right?"

"That about sums it up."

"What about vehicles?"

She frowned, having not considered that question. "We

have one SUV now for getting around. We'll need to have at least one armored SUV plus a couple of escorts available. Ideally, transport will be magical, but we can't count on it."

Zack nodded. He slipped on a pair of glasses and waggled his rings in front of them. A moment later, he started gesturing.

Danica asked, "What are you doing?"

He turned as if surprised. "Oh. You don't have glasses or a lens. Okay, here." He pulled a box out of his pocket and tossed it to her.

She donned the flimsy pair of glasses it contained and saw an image floating in midair, a layout of the interior as seen from above. As Zack moved his fingers, his rings glowed in her augmented vision, and things appeared on the map. An area was shaded in with crosshatching and labeled Garage, right next to the two large roll-up doors in the far side wall.

She asked, "What's that about a lens?"

"It's a new thing Arthur's been testing. A contact lens that does the same things as the display glasses. You have to wear a small belt pack since it can't store the supporting hardware in the frame like the glasses, but it's much less noticeable."

"Put those on the list, for sure."

Zack rubbed his hands together. "I'm in heaven. All right, we'll need an area for planning, one for labs and fabrication, and somewhere for our infomancer to live." Areas were highlighted on the floor plan as he said each word. "We will have infomancer support of our own, right? Not timesharing or anything?"

That was a question she had considered. "We will, but

we'll probably have to be freelance at first, depending on when the first job comes in. Arthur and I have a client meeting tomorrow, so we might be improvising a bit if we get the gig."

Zack laughed. "Improvising is what I do best."

Jilly had been watching everything from Danica's shoulder. "What is he doing?" Danica lifted her glasses and held them in front of Jilly's face so she could see. "Oh. Pretty."

She leapt off Danica's shoulder and flew around the space. Danica put the glasses back on as Zack colored in another space.

He explained, "This will be the equipping area for the team, and we'll put storage right next to it." By the time he finished, he had most of the layout covered, all of it served by a central corridor that stretched through the currently empty part of the building.

Danica pointed at an unmarked space. "What's that?"

"Expansion. No telling what we'll need, right?" He walked toward the assembly line and waved his hand some more. In the AR display, pieces of equipment received labels and descriptions. He shook his head. "I don't know that I can do anything useful with this stuff."

"I don't think you need to. I'll check with Arthur, but I'm pretty sure he doesn't have any plans for it."

"How strong is your magic?"

She frowned at the question. "I'm sorry?"

He turned to face her. "I've known a lot of magicals. Some of them could lift a car, say, and others could lift a truck carrying a *bunch* of cars. Which end are you near?"

"As long as I'm well-rested and haven't overdone it

recently, closer to the latter. I've never really tested it out to the maximum, but I've also never failed to lift anything when I made the attempt."

Zack scratched the back of his neck. "So, say, if we undid the bolts holding some of these things into the floor, you might be able to push them all away to give us more room?"

"Probably. I can't guarantee it. I'm sure we'll add more magicals to the team as we go along, and we can work together on it if I can't handle it alone. Plan as if we can do it, but not right away."

"Good. I'd like to put in some training stuff. Maybe a configurable obstacle-slash-shooting course. I don't know how well that would work. We might have to see if there's a place around here that does it."

"Does what?"

"Obstacle courses for training. Like maybe a paintball place we could work with. I'm guessing you'll want to take your team out now and again to work on your skills, right?"

Danica could already tell that keeping up with Zack's high-speed train of thought would be a challenge. "That's true."

Zack grinned. "I want to come along on those. I know I generally won't be in the field, but I'd like to be *able* to be in the field, if you know what I mean."

She chuckled darkly. "Given that it's you, me, and Jilly right now, you might find yourself in the field sooner than you expect."

"I can live with that."

The dragon landed on Danica's shoulder in a flutter of

wings. She gestured upward with one wing, and Danica followed the move toward the girders far above. Jilly advised, "I'll need a bed up there. Something soft and comfy. Plus, this whole place needs to be cleaned. It's dusty." As if to emphasize the point, she let out a small sneeze.

Danica laughed. "Well, all right then. Magic is good for that. I have a special spell that works like a tornado to suck dust right out the door."

Jilly twitched her wings in what Danica was coming to realize was a happy motion. "I can't wait to see it."

Zack added, "Me either, that sounds cool."

Danica grinned. Her team was coming along quite well already. "Well then, let's get to it."

CHAPTER TWELVE

The next morning, Danica dressed in more formal business attire, which meant slightly higher heels on her boots and a nicer blouse under her suit, then portaled to Miami. Arthur introduced her to one of the other members of Spellbound's team, a witch who was Miami's primary investigator.

Rose was blonde, pretty, chipper, and well-dressed. Her handshake was solid, and a bit of mirth in her eyes told Danica she knew she was pretty and played it up so others would underestimate her. They exchanged pleasantries. Then Rose opened a portal for them.

Arthur stepped through and Danica followed. Just like that, they were in New York City, somewhere surrounded by lots of skyscrapers. Danica turned in a circle, staring upward at the massive structures.

He asked, "First time?"

Danica laughed. "Yeah, actually. I've always been more of a West Coast or Chicago girl. Never got quite this far northeast for anything other than an airport connection."

"Well, this is where our next potential client is, Rokket-tfuel Records." He started walking.

She fell into step beside him. "I've heard of them. They have some really big names, everything from K-pop to boy bands to EDM."

"They do. They also have a problem."

"Which is?"

He stopped at a building and pulled open a door for her. "Something we'll discover shortly, together." The lobby featured glass walls on all sides that let in slashes of sunlight where they could make it through the surrounding buildings. Some intersected with the circular reception desk in the middle as they approached it.

Arthur said some things that passed over Danica's ears unheeded as she stared around at the various sculptures inside, which featured major sports stars, movie stars, and musicians. She muttered, "It's like a celebration of celebrity."

Arthur laughed. "You'll probably see that more often than you think from now on. Better get used to it. No one wants a starstruck security expert."

"Jilly would love flying around in here." She'd left the dragon with Zack, who was overseeing some work in the warehouse. Arthur had arranged for contractors to come in and do the more complicated work, demonstrating again that his list of connections was quite prodigious and wide-ranging.

They rode upward in an elevator with no buttons that stopped at the seventy-fourth floor.

A receptionist stepped out from behind the desk to greet them and escorted them to a conference room. After ensuring they were properly supplied with tea in Arthur's case and coffee in hers, the receptionist slid a silver tray with a variety of sweets on it near them and left the room. Danica took a chocolate chip cookie and nibbled on it. "I could definitely get used to this kind of treatment. I feel almost fancy."

Arthur replied, "I guess when you're in the big leagues you have to act like it."

"Is this kind of thing your goal?" She waved the cookie at the room around them.

He picked up a cookie and sniffed it. "Too opulent for me. No matter how big we get, I like things a little smaller, less this." He gestured at their surroundings, which had a full wall of windows looking out at the New York skyline, mahogany furniture, and a conference table that probably cost more than the average American salary and could seat a dozen and a half.

A man in a dark suit walked in, trailed by another who was an assistant, to judge by the tablet in his hands that he tapped on as he walked in. The man introduced himself as Logan Gould and took a seat. He pulled his cuffs one after the other in what had to be habit. "So, we have a problem."

Arthur replied, "That much I know. I hope we can help you. Who is it?"

The man sighed. "Damien Zane."

Danica managed not to cough on her coffee only with an effort of will. She swallowed. "The megastar?"

Gould raised an eyebrow. "The same. He'll be doing a few warmup gigs in arenas before embarking on the stadium tour. We'll have ordinary security in place, but we want an extra layer of protection until a certain situation sorts itself out."

Arthur asked, "What situation?"

"This one." He nodded at his assistant and the table's surface turned into a video display. One after the other, videos of people making threats against Zane appeared. Some were downright violent. Others seemed desperate for attention.

When they finished, Gould explained, "They're from anonymous social media accounts. We sent infomancers after the details, but they couldn't find any, which is a red flag."

Danica asked, "Why go after him?"

Gould shrugged. "Any of the usual possibilities are in play, from someone who erroneously believes they're in a relationship with him, to those who want to kidnap him for money, to those who think he should no longer be among the living for one reason or another."

Arthur sipped his tea and mused, "All of this stuff taken together feels like someone with experience is behind it. It's strange they'd want to telegraph it like this."

Gould nodded. "That's exactly what my contact in the FBI said, too. He thought it might be a psychological ploy, but we don't want to take any chances."

Arthur asked, "How big a team?"

"Whatever's necessary. I trust you to handle the details. You come very highly recommended. We'll have the main security at the shows covered. I want a little extra under-cover protection near him in case the regular amount isn't enough."

Arthur looked at her. "Danica?"

She looked at Gould. "How serious does your FBI contact think this is?"

"He said we should consider it as a credible threat to his life."

"All right then." She looked at her boss. "Are there any rules we have to play by in that situation?"

Arthur shrugged. "Only the usual. Defend yourself, defend your principal. You're cleared to hit first if a valid threat is present, but you can't shoot anyone who looks at you, or him, funny, either."

Gould added, "While protecting him, you must also be careful to protect his reputation. We can't afford to be roughing up his fans or anything. But like I said, his existing security crew should be adequate for that task. You'll be there for anything unexpected."

Danica considered the angles, then confirmed, "Okay. We can do this."

Arthur replied, "I'm confident you can. Gould?"

"As am I. Thomas here can act as your interface and handle the details." He stood and extended a hand. "Thanks so much. I look forward to working with you."

Arthur shook his hand, and as she did the same, Danica asked, "How much influence will we have over Damien's activities?"

Gould laughed, and even Thomas abandoned his neutral expression to smile at the question. "None. He's a rock star. Expect him to act like one."

As Gould left the room, Danica shook her head. "Awesome."

Arthur patted her on the shoulder consolingly. "If I hadn't thought you perfectly able to handle this type of nuanced situation, I wouldn't have hired you." She was pretty sure she heard laughter behind his words.

Thomas informed them, "The first gig is a week away, although rehearsals are already underway. I imagine you want to meet with him soon, though."

Danica nodded. "Yeah. Let's set it up for as early as reasonable so I can get the lay of the land and figure out how we'll best fit in."

"Credentials won't be a problem. Just tell me how many. I'll make sure you have full access."

Arthur asked, "How does Damien feel about this?"

Thomas's smile returned. "He doesn't know. Mr. Gould figured it would be best if you all told him."

Danica laughed again, shook her head, and pinched the bridge of her nose. "Awesome."

CHAPTER THIRTEEN

Once they were back in the lobby of the record label's building, Danica opened the portal to the office in Miami, and they stepped through. Arthur said, "I have another recommendation for you."

He'd told her to clear the day of other obligations, so this didn't come as a complete surprise. "Okay. Who is it?"

"Alexandra Hawthorne. Former military. Serious badass."

"Sounds like the kind of person you might want under-cover near a rock star."

He nodded emphatically. "Exactly the type of person. She'll be useful in other situations too, of course. But if you have a client with attitude, she, like you, isn't going to shy away from calling him on his nonsense."

Danica liked the sound of that. "Perfect. I'm guessing you set up a meet already?"

"Yeah." He gestured her toward a part of the office she hadn't been in. "You'll have to grab some work clothes before we go."

She looked down at herself and confirmed she was still properly dressed after the business meeting. "You might not have noticed, but I'm wearing work clothes. This isn't exactly my loungewear."

He chuckled. "Not the right kind for this type of work." He took her to the company's uniform storage closet. At his recommendation, she selected some simple canvas cargo pants, a tank top, and a heavy canvas shirt with the Spellbound Security logo. She found a pair of boots that didn't fit too badly and threw them into a bag with the clothes, which she tossed in the back of his SUV.

Arthur drove for about a half-hour, leaving the suburban area that was home to his office. They wound up in an area with structures that were notably more spread out from each other and surrounded by land. Some were perfectly green, but others were baked to a dull brown by the sun. He took a turn and pulled up to a gate in a tall chain fence topped with razor wire, then held out his ID to the camera mounted there.

The gate opened, and Danica observed, "You're so important. So fancy."

He laughed. "Oh yes, definitely."

They drove for another minute before the tree-lined road opened onto a parking lot beside a huge clearing. Danica thought it looked like a farm, although she wasn't sure what they might grow in the Miami heat. He pulled up near a group of people standing about a hundred yards away from a Cape Cod-style house in the clearing.

A better look at the group revealed eight people in body armor with riot helmets under their arms listening to a woman speaking urgently. Danica caught a few words as they got out of the car, then the woman yelled, "Deploy." Those in body armor ran for the house as the woman approached them. She stuck out her hand, and Arthur shook it.

He greeted her. "Alexandra."

The other woman nodded at Danica with intense dark eyes. "This her?" Arthur nodded in confirmation. "Doesn't seem like much." A smile softened the playful insult.

The woman wore fatigue bottoms and an Army T-shirt that showed off her muscled arms. Short brown hair fit perfectly with the martial image. Her left forearm had a faint scar that caught Danica's eye because it seemed the only imperfect thing about her.

Arthur replied, "Appearances can be deceiving."

Danica interjected, "You know, I'm right here. I can hear you."

Alexandra chuckled. "Get changed."

She looked around. "Where?"

The chuckle turned into a laugh. "In the car. Don't worry, we won't look." The other woman grabbed Arthur's arm and turned him away from the car. Danica grumbled, failed to come up with a useful insult to throw back at her, and complied.

When Danica rejoined them, Alexandra handed her a rifle that had been strapped across her back, then unbuckled her gun belt and handed it over. As Danica put it on, Alexandra explained, "You're taking my role. There's a principal in the building the SWAT unit is defending. Your job is to get in and take them out."

Danica cinched the belt tight. "You're teaching SWAT to defend? Is that within their wheelhouse?"

"I'm giving them an opportunity to see the process from the other side. It will provide a useful perspective when they plan for missions."

Danica nodded and pulled the pistol from its holster. It was larger than usual, painted bright green, and had a curved magazine mounted to the top. The whole arrangement made it look like a space weapon. "Range?"

"About what you get with an ordinary rifle and handgun. They're paintballs. Face shots are off-limits, by the way."

She pushed the gun back into its holster with a nod. "Any other rules?"

"No offensive magic. No using shields to pretend you didn't get hit. Although you can shield your face and head as long as you acknowledge if you get hit there."

"I'm not likely to cheat."

Alexandra shrugged. "Didn't think you would. Rules are rules, no matter who they're for."

Danica looked at Arthur. "If I get humiliated, I'm coming back and shooting you from head to toe with paintballs."

He laughed. "I have every faith in you, Danica."

She muttered, "That's one of us," as she moved toward the battlefield. The distance was long enough that they wouldn't have a good eye on her unless they used binoculars. Still, she dropped into the longish grass as soon as she was far enough in. It would've been about thigh height to walk through, which meant it should provide the cover she'd need to get close. Trained eyes would probably see it shift as she moved through it, no matter how slow she was, but she hoped her opponents wouldn't be that alert.

She already had one crucial piece of information. Her enemies numbered only eight. It gave her an advantage to know that, although the lack of real weapons negated it somewhat. In an actual fight, her magical shields or body armor would provide a defense against their bullets. If she got hit with a paintball here, it was over, unlike in the real world, where she was sure one opportunity would be all she'd need to take someone down.

Danica chided herself for letting her mind wander, lay still for a moment, then reached inward for her magic. No offensive magic and no shields still left her with a lot of options. She figured using illusion to hide herself was too borderline, although she could make a case that it wasn't "offensive" magic. The SWAT team deserved the most realistic experience possible, or the most realistic one it could get under the unlikely scenario of a single attacker against a fully defended building.

She used the magic to enhance all her senses and to give her a little extra spring in her step. Nothing unrealistic, just what adrenaline would give her during a fight. At eight on one, a little hedge was appropriate. She lifted her head enough to see over the grass, and her enhanced vision showed her the scene in detail.

Defenders were positioned front, side, and back from her perspective, plus one at the back corner she could see, and presumably another matching it opposite at the front, leaving two inside. Luckily for her, the building had no windows on its upper story where a lookout might spot her. It struck her again that eight versus one without full use of her magic was a little daunting.

Danica would have problems if they stacked up on the

inside where she'd have no ability to dodge. Their numbers were sufficient to make a human wall around the target and shoot her as she came in. Since that wouldn't be in the spirit of the scenario, she doubted they would do it. It was clear that she had to improve the odds before she breached the house.

She considered what she might do if she could use her magic fully. Her first plan would be to veil and sneak up, but if that wasn't available, she'd use magic to create a distraction away from her position. She could've made grass in another area move like she was passing through it, which would have drawn the eyes of the defenders. Since that wasn't an option, she searched the ground for some hand-size rocks and started crawling when the breeze moved the grass.

When she got to a good distance, Danica threw the rocks low and away from her position in the hope it would pull eyes from her. She used a touch of magic to throw them a little farther away. Non-offensive and a legitimate response to the odds.

Her enhanced hearing caught the team talking to one another, but she couldn't distinguish the words. Their tactical radios meant they didn't have to yell, and while her enhanced hearing was good, it wasn't good enough to bring her information from eighty yards away.

She stayed low and kept moving when the breeze stirred or when one of her rocks distracted them. In an ideal world, she'd have Jilly with her to give her warnings if any of her actions drew attention. She smiled fondly at the thought of her companion and discovered that she missed having her around already, although they hadn't been apart for a full day. Something about the fae dragon was warming and relaxing. She wondered if that was part of the dragon's innate magic and made a mental note to ask. There was a lot she didn't know about Jilly.

Danica clamped down on her wandering thoughts with a muttered curse at herself and growled, "All right. Let's do some damage."

CHAPTER FOURTEEN

Danica paused to reassess when she was within fifteen yards of the edge of the well-kept grass surrounding the house. From her position at the side of the structure, she could see one guard directly in the middle of the space ahead and another at the corner that bounded that side in the back. She'd lost sight of the ones in the front and back of the building as she moved closer.

She expected the building would only have doors in the front and back since one wasn't visible on the side. Her instincts told her the natural inclination would be to watch the front more carefully, so she decided to go in from the back. That meant she'd have to deal with the two in view and probably one more to get in.

It wouldn't be easy since they were sure to be on guard. If she had full use of her magic, she would've dampened sound and lightning-blasted the one in front of her to take him out without anyone else noticing. Since that wasn't allowed, she needed to create a distraction at the back that would hopefully draw the corner one away so she could engage the side one.

Once she took the first down, she would be in the land of improvisation since she couldn't hide them. That was fine. She was good at it.

Danica hefted her last rock and used some extra magic to throw it high and far. It clattered to the ground beyond the back of the building. The guard at the corner moved as she'd hoped, and she lifted her rifle, aimed down the sights, and fired a paintball square into the chest of the guard on the side.

Danica relocated immediately, falling to her chest and scrambling toward the back. She hoped people would think the distraction in the back meant she'd come from the front, although she was well aware that particular hope was a reach. Now they had a decision to make. Would the person from the corner come up to take the side, in which case she'd take him out too since there was no one to see it, or would he stay at the corner?

They chose a different option. Someone came from the front of the house to take the post at the side. That almost caused her to change her plans since the front might now be less well-defended. A frontal assault didn't feel right, so she decided to continue with her current plan.

Danica made her way through the grass slowly, some-times moving only a foot or two in a minute. She looked up every so often to see how people were positioned. The ones in the rear were alert, systematically scanning their fields of fire through the scopes of their rifles. Infrared scopes would have found her, but she figured that would be too great an advantage in this scenario.

What would really tilt the odds would be a couple of flash-bang grenades. One into the back, and I'm through the defenders in an instant, then one inside, and Bob's your uncle.

Well, that wouldn't be much for a training exercise for the SWAT team, which no doubt explained why she didn't have grenades. She set those fanciful wishes aside and focused on the moment. She would have to take the pair in quick sequence so they couldn't shout a warning that would bring another around the back.

The door was closed, presumably bolted. She'd give it a hard kick, but if that didn't work, she'd blast it off with magic. Strictly speaking, that wouldn't be offensive as long as it didn't hit anybody.

Danica reached down to ensure her pistol was loose in its holster and readied herself to move. Her instinct told her to put more magic into her muscles and increase her speed dramatically. She would in a real scenario, but that was outside the parameters Alexandra had given her.

She wondered for a moment how the other woman would've handled this assault and judged she would have done much the same. She probably would have been smart enough to pick off more of them before going in, but today Danica lacked the patience for that.

She muttered, "All right, here we go." She moved to her knees and lifted the rifle to take an aimed shot, but a shout caused her to lurch into motion. While she'd focused on the two at the back, the one on the side had moved to get an angle on her. She snapped her barrel around at him and pulled the trigger. His paintball whirred past her head as she fell to the ground and rolled to the side. She came up to see that hers had struck him in the shoulder.

The pair in the back stared at her. She pulled the trigger spasmodically and swept the rifle horizontally across them. Somehow, she missed the first, putting paint splotches on the house to either side of him. She nailed the second in the thigh, and the man dropped his gun and fell to the ground with an annoyed curse.

She lurched into a run parallel to the house as paintballs flew through the air behind her, her slightly augmented speed enough to cause the shots to miss. She brought her rifle back around to point back toward the one shooting at her as another came around from the far side of the house. She snarled at the realization they'd set a trap for her, and she'd walked into it.

Danica pulled the trigger three times and struck her target, the man originally at the back corner, then hit the quick release for the rifle and threw the weapon at the newcomer. The unexpected move startled him. She raced forward as she pulled her pistol from the holster.

He knocked the rifle aside with his, then leveled it at her. She had gotten her pistol free but was almost into hand-to-hand range. He fired, and she slid on the rocky ground to dodge the paintball. Stones chewed up the side of her leg as they cut through the canvas pants, but she ignored it, kicked the man's legs out from under him, and used force magic to cushion his fall. She shot him in the chest with her pistol.

Shouts came from all around as she popped back up to her feet. He swiped a kick at her legs, which was cheating, but the blow only slightly redirected her. Her boot slammed into the door handle and broke the wood. The door popped open, and she raised her pistol, spotted the principal in the corner of the single large room, and pulled the trigger.

Her paint pellet hit him just before two others from the guards inside struck her. Alexandra walked in the front door and shouted, "It's over. Holster weapons."

Everyone complied, and one of the SWAT members who'd shot her came over to Danica and announced, "You're dead."

She accepted his hand and shook it. She nodded at his protectee. "So is your objective."

He turned and grunted. "Damn."

Alexandra laughed. "Damn is right. Everyone gather up your stuff, and we'll debrief outside."

A couple of hours later, after Danica had portaled home, showered, and changed, she met Arthur again at the exercise location. They chatted amiably while they waited for Alexandra to appear.

She came out dressed in boots, jeans, and a faded T-shirt. "Let's go talk. I'll drive." Arthur protested, but she corralled him and convinced him to get into the back seat, then aggressively drove to a nearby bar.

A neon sign proclaimed Frank's, and a neon martini glass went from vertical to a forty-five-degree angle underneath it. The parking lot was dirt and rock, and a small cloud of dust spewed up as Alexandra slammed the brakes to skid perfectly into a parking spot.

The interior was loud, full of laughter and random noises. Billiard balls smacked into one another, darts landed on boards, and competitive trash-talking accompanied it. Alexandra exchanged high-fives and handshakes with several people as she led Danica and Arthur to a corner booth and sat.

A server appeared almost instantly, dressed in cowboy boots, short jeans shorts, and a midriff top. Alexandra requested, "LaRubia all around."

The server replied, "No draft today, just bottles."

"Fine." They chatted about the place. Alexandra pointed out people she knew and where she knew them from until their drinks came. Then they clinked bottles and sipped. Alexandra put hers on the table. "You did good today."

Danica shrugged. "I had the advantage. They were busy worrying about their protectee."

"What magic did you use?"

She raised an eyebrow. "Nothing out of bounds. A little sensory buffing, a little extra strength for rock throwing."

Alexandra looked thoughtful. "What would you have done if you'd had full access?"

"Snuck up invisibly to each to take them down one by one or in pairs when they were too close together to avoid it. Sound buffer so no one would hear."

"That would be a good plan."

Arthur asked, "What do you think?"

Alexandra shrugged. "I think she's as good as you said she was."

Danica frowned. "Doesn't this normally work the other way around? Like, the person being hired demonstrates their ability to the person doing the hiring?"

Arthur laughed. "Usually. But you said you trusted me. And I'm telling you, Alexandra is worth it. She'll be a great addition."

"Well, who am I to argue? It was a fun game to play. You're in?"

Alexandra grinned. "Yeah. I think I am."

CHAPTER FIFTEEN

The next morning, Danica dressed in boots, casual jeans, and a loose button-down, then opened a portal from her front yard to the street outside Alexandra's apartment. Alexandra came out right on time, and her gaze went first to the fae dragon perched on Danica's shoulder. "Well, who might you be?"

The dragon replied, "Jilly. Danica is my human."

Alexandra's gaze slid to her, and Danica grinned. "It's true. I am. She's made that abundantly clear." A small flex of claws pinched her enough to convey Jilly's amusement.

Alexandra nodded. "Well. That's cool. Seems like the workplace will be interesting, at least."

Danica let out a bark of laughter. "You can say that, I think." She opened a portal to the office and gave Alexandra the tour. Then they took scooters down to the opposite end.

Alexandra asked, "How do they get back to the other side?"

Danica shrugged. "Either they get there by people riding them, or I take them through by a portal."

"Portal travel is so convenient."

"It definitely is, as long as you don't do it wrong and wind up in the World In Between. I thought you'd like to see the tunnel between the offices, which is why I didn't bring us straight here." She punched the code into the door's keypad and headed inside as it slid aside.

Someone deeper in the building yelled, "Be careful. Give the robots a chance to sense you before you start moving fast."

The warehouse was full of activity. Robots of every kind, some humanoid and others very much not, moved through the space, building walls, shifting boxes around, and generally turning the place into the facility Zack had envisioned.

He handed them hard hats. "Maybe shield Jilly. There's some stuff going on above us."

Danica looked up and saw robots whipping along the girders using tools of various kinds for tasks she couldn't begin to guess. She extended her power to put shields around them all. "All right. Looks good."

He shrugged. "It's coming along. Let's go into the one room that's finished, more or less." They passed some human workers as Zack took them into the room designated as a storage area on the initial layout plan. It had several chairs inside, and they each took one.

Jilly leaned against Danica's neck and burrowed her head in. Danica looked down to see that the dragon's eyes had closed and she was curled up. She lifted a finger to stroke the dragon. "All right. We're getting started a little earlier than I expected. I thought we'd have a bigger team when our first client showed up."

Zack interrupted, "I'm sorry. I'm Zack. Who are you?"

Alexandra laughed. "Alexandra. Protector type."

"Tech type." He looked at Danica. "You can continue, rude person."

Danica laughed. "Why thank you, tech type. We're meeting Damien Zane, codename Rockstar, tomorrow morning. He's doing a television appearance, an outdoor concert thing. We're keeping an eye on him as part of our gig protecting him."

Alexandra observed, "This seems like a bad idea."

Danica nodded in agreement. "From what Arthur has told me, a lot of our gigs will be bad ideas, often with people who won't behave in any kind of self-protective way."

Alexandra rolled her eyes. "Fantastic. Too late to resign?"

"Yep, you're stuck with us now. Zack, what kind of equipment do we have?"

He rubbed his hands together. "Ah, one of my favorite subjects." He crossed to the cabinet that was the room's only furniture other than the chairs, took out boxes, and handed them out. Danica opened hers and found a pair of glasses and earpieces inside.

He explained, "Data display glasses and comm earpieces. For now, I can handle routing data. In the future, we'll probably want an infomancer on hand for that kind of stuff, someone who's better with computers than I.

"The earpiece can be controlled from the base station here, and we can set up multiple channels or interface with others. It automatically picks up whatever you say through bone conductivity, so you don't have to worry about ambient noise. If you're in a particularly noisy situation, you can wear two to block both ears." He seemed quite pleased when he finished the recitation.

Danica replied, "Not sure what we'll face tomorrow. Why don't we take a pair each, just in case."

Alexandra laughed. "I was going to suggest the same thing. Great minds and all that."

Zack said, "That takes care of comms and intel."

Alexandra asked, "Do we have any kind of overwatch on the site?"

Danica replied, "Nothing other than what Rockstar's team can give us."

"We should have more."

Zack added, "I couldn't agree more, Alexandra."

She grinned. "Since we're teammates you can call me Alex, as long as you're not a jerk about it."

He laughed. "I think I can manage not to be a jerk."

"In my experience, that seems difficult for your gender."

Zack put a hand on his chest and laughed. "Ouch."

Danica laughed and raised her hand, and Alexandra high-fived her. Danica asked, "What about body armor?"

He shook his head. "This is coming too fast for anything other than off-the-shelf, and I'm not sure how you'd hide it. I have a hookup to get custom-made gear, really good stuff, but not in time for tomorrow."

Danica nodded. "Okay, put that together as soon as you can. We'll manage tomorrow."

Alexandra asked, "Weapons?"

He returned to the cabinet and took out a pair of cases.

He propped them open and placed them on the women's laps. Inside were Glock 19 automatic pistols, fifteen-round magazines, and boxes of ammunition. "Since you'll be in a crowd, frangible bullets make sense. You don't want to shoot through your target and hit an innocent behind them. I think this will be the case for most of what you do. They make big holes, but if you're shooting, that's probably what you want, right?"

Danica opened the box. "Standard rounds."

Zack grunted in annoyance. "Despite my advice to the contrary, Arthur doesn't use anti-magic ammunition by default. I'll have some here in reasonably short order but getting them in frangible is always a challenge."

Alexandra racked the slide on the weapon and nodded. "They'll do. We'll need to test them out at the range."

He nodded. "We'll have a range here, maybe, if we can get all that equipment out of the way. For now, there's a commercial range in town."

Danica praised, "You've done good work, Zack."

"And I'm not done yet." He went back to the cabinet and came out with two metal rods. He handed one to each of them.

Danica stood, stepped back, and gave the object a practiced flick. It extended to full length. "Asp?"

Zack nodded. "Newer model. It has a battery in the handle capable of delivering a Taser charge at the tip."

Alexandra asked, "Just one?"

"Unfortunately. Once we're up and running, I'll see if I can make that better."

Alexandra extended hers to full length and worked through a quick set of strikes. "Great balance." She hit the retract button and pushed the weapon closed. "This'll do for tomorrow once we get a little more surveillance on the place."

Zack said, "I'm not sure what you're thinking about blending in, but his security is all in dark suits, trying to look menacing like they're Secret Service or something."

Danica replied, "We want to be as undercover as possible for this one, I think."

Zack nodded. "I thought that might be the case, so I got some pictures. Their crew dresses in all black too, but cargo pants, tennis shoes, and big button-down shirts over T-shirts. Some of them wear the button-downs open. Some fasten them all the way up. I can have replicas made."

"All right. Do what you can to get us some eyes for tomorrow and whip up the outfits. We'll spend some time at the range, then recon the site."

CHAPTER SIXTEEN

The next morning, Danica donned her crew clothes for the concert. Looking at herself in the mirror, she thought the ensemble looked pretty good. "Maybe I need to switch to wearing all black all the time."

Jilly was a bright ball of color on her shoulder. She spread her wings. "Black is boring. You should be a rainbow."

Danica laughed. "That might be pushing it a little far, my friend. Let's test your hiding spot." She unbuttoned a couple of buttons and held her shirt open. Whoever Zack had gotten the clothes from had sewn a pocket inside to hold the dragon. She nestled inside it with her head sticking out, and Danica re-buttoned the shirt. "Can you see?"

"A little. I like this. It's cozy. I can nap."

Danica laughed. "We're working today."

"You're working. I'm napping." Fake snoring came from inside her shirt, and she patted the small one.

"Of course. What was I thinking." She slipped on her

glasses, put in her earpiece, and announced, "Danica, online."

Alexandra replied immediately. "About time. I've been waiting."

Danica's eyes flicked up to the time display in the corner of her glasses. "I still have one minute."

"Didn't anyone ever tell you that five minutes early was on time?"

"No. Because on time is on time. It's right there in the words."

Alexandra snorted in derision. "You'd never make it in the Army."

Danica opened the portal. "Why do I think I'm gonna hear that a lot?"

She stepped through and saw the other woman smiling. "Because it's true?"

Jilly faked an extra loud snore, and Alexandra raised an eyebrow. Danica shook her head. "We're working. She is napping. Dramatically." A small laugh emerged from under the canvas.

Zack greeted, "Morning, everyone. I'm adding in Voltaic."

A female voice with a synthesized edge responded, "Hello, people. Feed incoming."

Danica asked, "You're not *the* Voltaic, are you?"

The infomancer chuckled. "If there's another, I'd have to kill them."

"I watch your streams pretty often. You're one of the best gamers I've ever seen."

"Why, thank you. And before you ask, no, I don't cheat and use my magic. Just hard-won skill."

Zack added, "And maybe an affinity for it because you think like a computer and spend every waking minute interfacing with one."

Voltaic played a sound file from *Doctor Who*. "Exterminate."

Everyone laughed. A moment later, images popped into Danica's display in small windows on the left and right. Either she guessed Danica's preferences or had already talked with Zack about it.

Four small windows showed camera angles on the stage. The infomancer explained, "On the left are direct feeds from the network's cameras." A window opened on the right to show an overhead view. "That's my drone. It's way high up because local authorities are pretty touchy about flying a drone around when there's a megastar below."

Alexandra asked, "Is that the adoring tone of a Damien Zane fan I hear in your voice?"

Voltaic snorted. "Hardly. I don't like the pretty boys much."

"I hear his personality doesn't match his looks."

"I hear the same."

Alexandra asked, "Shall we find out?"

Danica fished out their credentials, put one lanyard over her head, and handed the other to Alexandra. She opened a portal, and they crossed the distance to New York City. The stage was only a few blocks away, and the holding area for the artist was in a group of trailers nearby. Their credentials got them into the restricted area, then shouting drew them on.

Their first glimpse of Damien was of him pulling off his

shirt and throwing it at a woman who was presumably a wardrobe assistant. He was scrawny, as if he regularly forgot to eat. Another shirt was procured, and he pulled it on. It was plain black, and Danica wondered what could've upset him about the other one.

Another pair of women bustled up behind him and inserted in-ear monitors into his ears with the cord trailing down to a small box they placed on the back of his belt. Alexandra asked, "Why have them wired at all?"

Voltaic replied, "Modern stage shows use lots of signals. Sometimes you need a lot of power to cut through all their noise. Artists complain because they're artists, but they know it's the right thing to do, and most of them are also professionals."

Damien snapped his fingers, and someone put a mug of coffee in his hand. He sipped from it, winced, then sipped from it again. His mood softened, and those around him relaxed accordingly.

Danica figured it was the right moment and walked up to him and extended a hand. "Danica Grey, Spellbound Security." He looked at the hand, then up at her, and made no attempt to take it. She let it drop. "We're here to provide additional protection."

He snorted. "You?" His English accent sounded lower-class rough to her ears, not that cultured upper-class pompous variety. Something from a smaller neighborhood, perhaps. "I'm sure I'll be fine. I have Vince and Victor." Two brawny men in suits nodded from their positions nearby.

Alexandra asked, "Do you only hire security whose names begin with V?"

"Clever. I hope your security skills are sharper than your wits."

Danica shook her head. He was everything she'd been warned to expect. "Anyway, if we tell you to do something, you do it. No questions. Understood?"

His smile said he'd do no such thing. "Sure, babe, whatever."

Danica resisted the urge to punch him and looked at the two V-men. "Same goes for you. We won't be on your security channel because we don't want to interfere with your operation, but our infomancer will listen in. We'll coordinate as needed. If we do interfere, believe that it's a real threat. Hopefully we won't talk at all."

Vince smiled. "I don't know, might be fun talking to you two."

"Trust me. You couldn't handle us." The man laughed, and she looked at Alexandra. They understood each other even if Rockstar wasn't on board.

Voltaic reported, "He'll be moving in one minute."

Danica looked at Alexandra. "Any last-minute tips or concerns?"

The other woman shook her head. "We've got this. I'm sure we're here for nothing, just like he thinks."

"I'd love to think that too. But Arthur's instincts are usually right, and he made sure we met with Zane before this event."

Alexandra's posture straightened slightly. "Got it. I hear you."

One of the female assistants who had helped with the wardrobe issue yelled, "Fifteen seconds to move."

Somebody took the cup out of Damien's hand and

strapped a guitar over his shoulders. He pulled the pick from the holder on the side and readied himself. The assistant counted down, and they all moved together.

A guard led the procession with Alexandra behind him. An assistant, Damien, another assistant, and Danica brought up the rear. The other three band members trailed her. She itched to pull the pistol from its holster at the base of her spine, but that would be inappropriate for a crew member. She took a deep breath, focused her mind, and readied herself for whatever lay ahead.

CHAPTER SEVENTEEN

Danica had been to concerts in big and small venues but had never experienced anything from this perspective. The sight of the crowd as they came around the corner of the stage, screaming and yelling, cheering and holding signs, all of their attention focused on Damien, was nothing short of breathtaking. At that moment, she understood the desire for celebrity like she never had before.

Maybe it was the drug Damien was high enough on that he didn't need food. Even the tiny amount she experienced from being at the edge of it was heady stuff.

She took her position at the front right corner of the stage as he screamed, "Good morning, New York," and played the opening chord of his most popular song. Her earpieces automatically dimmed the sound to a background level.

Alexandra reported, "In position."

Danica replied, "Same here." Her gaze flicked up to the

overhead view in her glasses to confirm her partner was where she was supposed to be, at the opposite corner.

The band's security had the venue's rear locked down, and a physical barrier at the back of the stage would prevent anyone from shooting Damien from behind. Alexandra was responsible for the left side of the stage and half of the front, while Danica was responsible for the other half of the front and the right side.

She began the practiced surveillance motion, sweeping her gaze over the crowd, then up to the buildings on the left, then back to the crowd, then up to the buildings on the right. She spent more time on the latter since those were her primary responsibilities but couldn't help looking at Alexandra's side as well. If she had to guess, she imagined the other woman was doing the same.

She didn't need to look back to see what was happening behind her. The four small windows on the left side of her visual field showed her the feeds from the cameras. His band included a drummer, a guitarist, and a bass player, all dressed in stereotypical rock star attire. Somehow this felt more casual than a "real" concert, maybe because it was outside or in the daylight. The band gave off the requisite energy to pump up the crowd.

Alexandra commented, "They're pretty good live."

Danica replied, "Most live music is good. Except jazz. I recognize it's an absolute failing in myself, but I just can't like jazz."

Alexandra laughed. "It's country for me. Well, new country. I like old country."

Voltaic interjected, "Must be difficult living in the South, then."

"Miami is not really the South. It's its own thing."

The chatter fell off as they all focused on their jobs again. They had concluded that the most dangerous times would be right at the start when the band came out or near the end. Those would be the moments of energy and confusion, and confusion benefited attackers.

Danica was distracted by Jilly wriggling against her chest. Eventually, the dragon stuck her head out between the buttons of her shirt. Danica asked, "Ready to work now, are you?"

Jilly yawned. "Yep." She clawed out of Danica's shirt, popping open one of the buttons to emerge, then launched herself into the air. A moment later, she was lost to sight.

Danica muttered, "I'm not feeling good about this."

Alexandra replied, "Me neither, although there's nothing that's calling out as a threat."

Voltaic added, "I don't see anything from above. Maybe it's the fact that your principal is standing out on a stage surrounded by throngs of people?"

Danica looked up. "And lots of windows. To hell with it. I'm going to shield him."

Zack reminded her, sounding reluctant, "His people told you not to do that."

"Best case, they won't even know. Worst case, they can fire us."

Alexandra let out a soft snort. "Trying to get us fired from our first gig?"

"With him involved? Maybe not that great a loss." She whispered the words and made small gestures with her fingers. She placed the shield at a small distance from his body and devoted one eye to watching the camera feed.

She'd have to draw the shield in if he did any of those rock star moves like going back-to-back with one of the other members while they played during a solo.

She was well-practiced at partitioning her mind to maintain multiple spells at a time. Her maximum was seven simultaneous spells, all of which required constant attention. She'd only managed it for about fifteen seconds before it had all fallen apart, much to the amusement of those who had dared her to try.

Voltaic called out each song on the setlist and how many remained. Finally, she reported, "*Laser Light Symphony*, last song. No encore."

Zack advised, "Watch out. Sometimes he jumps off the stage and goes along the barricade giving high-fives and stuff."

Via the camera windows, she watched him take off his guitar and throw it across the stage, where a stagehand caught it. Danica shook her head and thought the planning involved in pulling off a concert must be as complicated as planning an operation was for people like her.

Sure enough, as they reached the instrumental break in the song, Damien jumped down from the stage. She tightened the shield around him and removed his arms from it so there would be no barrier between him and the fans. She also took a few steps toward the center and noticed that Alexandra did the same across the way. She muttered, "Anything, Alex?"

The other woman replied, "No. Looks just like fans to me."

"If you see a weapon, call it out. I can magic it away from them."

"Affirmative."

His security was on either side of him, and they did a great job of controlling his interaction with the crowd. A few people tried to hang on, and they helped him disengage while he looked apologetic and basked in the love of his fans. Finally, he turned back toward the stage and one of his security people bent and made a cradle with his hands. Damien stepped into it, then flew to the stage as the man threw him.

He landed, turned, and threw up his hands. The crowd screamed its adoration, and he returned to the microphone for the last verse.

Alexandra muttered, "Thank goodness that's over."

Danica felt the same. "Right?"

A moment later, Jilly reported, *Open window. Near me.*

Danica always had a sense of where the dragon was and looked directly toward her. She saw the open window. It could be nothing, but it could also be something. She snapped, "Voltaic, window, stage right, probably thirty floors up."

The drone's camera spun and zoomed in. It spotted a rifle barrel well back from the window.

Everyone snapped, "Gun."

The weapon was too far away for Danica to hit it with her magic before the shot went off unless the person took all day about it. Instead, she used a blast of force magic to knock Damien down as the shot rang out. She slapped additional shields in front of each band member but was confident the bullet was meant for the star. It drilled into the back of the stage. His security swarmed him and took him out the back.

Danica shouted, "Alex, stay close to him."

The other woman replied, "Affirmative."

Voltaic reported, "The gun is gone."

Zack queried, "What are you going to do?"

Danica replied, "My superhero impersonation." She used a push of force magic to clear the panicked crowd and crew away from her, then slammed another burst into the ground and sent herself flying up toward the building.

CHAPTER EIGHTEEN

Danica's blast carried her over the crowd toward the building, but her power wasn't strong enough to get her there in one hop. She wasn't a superhero, only someone using the laws of magical physics to her advantage.

She landed on top of a light post and wobbled for a second before regaining her balance. Jilly hovered near the open window. Danica shouted, "What do you see?" Then she blasted toward the window on another rocket of force magic.

Jilly replied, *Hold on,* then flashed by the window. *Open door. No one inside that I saw.*

Danica's arc carried her toward where she wanted to go. She'd always been good at calculating the angles. She threw her right hand forward with the palm open and dispatched a burst of lightning. It shattered the upper window, and she crashed through the pane, rolled on the floor, and came up to one knee with her gun in her hand.

Jilly had been right. No one remained in the room. Blood flowed from several cuts on her hands and face, but they were shallow and didn't impede her grip or her vision. She announced, "Chasing him."

Jilly flashed by and into the hallway. After only a moment, she sent, *He's going up.*

"Then so am I."

Alexandra ran after the security team escorting Damien through the hidden door in the back of the stage. She had jumped onto the platform but had been cut off by the other band members as they made their escapes. Now she charged after her principal in the narrow backstage fenced-in area. Voltaic advised, "They're saying that as long as they can get to the trailer, they'll be safe."

Alexandra snapped, "Tell them that's stupid. He needs to be in a car on his way out of here. Or better, someone needs to portal him away."

"They don't have a magical on staff today."

"Idiots." She wouldn't have considered being responsible for a situation like this without some means of magical egress. They might have to discuss it with the team once they got Rockstar out of this situation. She broke out from the walkways into the area they'd been in earlier. Tour buses bounded it on two sides, and other vehicles blocked access to create a rectangle of relative safety.

She slowed to a walk and noted that an ambulance had pulled in where another vehicle had been and two male medics already had Damien in hand. They'd separated him from his security and had him sitting on a stretcher they'd pulled out from the ambulance. One administered oxygen while another put a blood pressure cuff around his wrist.

A third man, presumably the driver, called from inside the vehicle, "How is he?"

The other two exchanged glances. "We should take him in, just to be safe."

Vince stepped forward. "No. We'll call his personal physician. Unless his life is in imminent danger, he stays."

For a moment, Alexandra thought the guard's response was an overreaction. Then all three medics surged into motion. The one Vince was talking to stepped forward and delivered a punch to his solar plexus that knocked him backward, followed by a leaping back kick that knocked him sprawling on the ground. Alexandra winced as his head smacked off the ground with an audible *thwack*.

She reached under her shirt and pulled the Asp with her left hand as she drew the pistol with her right and charged. She realized the other two medics were already too close to her allies for her to take a shot, so she switched hands with the weapons as she ran forward.

Victor went down, leaving her with a clean shot at the medic. She thought of the Taser function and considered it would be good to have someone to ask about this attack, so instead of whipping a strike at his head, she poked the Asp out, almost like a fencer with a foil, and triggered the blast.

The medic dodged, wasting her effort, and spun into a kick. She fell and went into a backward somersault to avoid the attack and came up with her gun ready. The medic used the moment to grab Damien and drag him toward the ambulance. When he tried to struggle, an injector pressed to his neck rendered him boneless.

The other medic raced at her. She calculated the angles, took a step to the left so a miss wouldn't hit Damien, and pulled the trigger three times.

The first two bullets slammed into his chest, and the third buried itself in his forehead. That one wouldn't get up. She shifted her attention to the ambulance, but the back doors were closed, and she couldn't risk shooting blind through them. As she ran toward it, she shoved her pistol in its holster and growled, "Track the ambulance."

Danica called, "What ambulance?"

Alexandra barked, "Don't worry. I've got it."

Danica worried but focused on her opponent. Jilly gave her directions, and more than once warned her that her foe was lying in wait around a corner. She delayed during those times, then continued to pursue as he made his way to the roof.

She was surprised he hadn't brought magical support and wondered if this wasn't related to the online threats but was some random wacko. That threat had seemed organized and planned, as Arthur had pointed out. The long-range shot seemed anything but.

When she reached the final corridor, Jilly sent, *He went out the door.*

Danica replied, "Thanks, Jilly." She'd been carrying her pistol, hoping for a long-range shot at his legs, but put it away in favor of her Asp. She flicked the weapon to extend it and twirled it in her hand. Then she summoned her magic and allowed it to build before casting a veil around herself and running headlong at the door.

Before she arrived, she sent a force blast at it that knocked it off its hinges and sent it flying. A loud curse and a scuffle told her it struck the man. She stopped short before exiting the hallway and waited for a reaction.

None came, so she carefully moved out onto the roof. The man was half behind a piece of HVAC equipment but had his rifle trained on the door. She'd come through in a crouch in case he had some way to see her, but fortunately her veil worked as it was supposed to. She walked to the left, hoping to get a better angle to blast him with lightning and knock him out, but some instinct warned him.

He swiveled the gun and pulled the trigger. She dove out of the way, and the round deflected from her shield. She rolled and came up, then allowed herself to become visible. She smiled at the man, reinforced her shields, and walked toward him. "Let's have a chat, you and I."

He backpedaled and fired at her again, shaking his head. She realized she was being stupid since for all she knew he had anti-magic rounds in the magazine as well as the standard ones he'd fired so far. She reached out, wrapped force magic around the barrel, and ripped the gun out of his grip. The strap pulled him forward before it snapped, and he went down on his face.

Danica ran toward him, but he got up and dashed away toward the edge of the building. She feared he would jump, but a portal opened a few steps in front of him, proving he had magical support after all.

She snarled, "Oh, no you don't," and crafted her force magic into a rope she sent whipping across the space between them. It wrapped around his ankle, and he went down. She pulled him back through just in time to avoid the portal's closure. Having a portal close while you were in it was not good since whatever part of you was on each side stayed there.

She looked down at him. "Not getting away that easy, moron." He moved as if to get up, and she blasted him with lightning magic until he stopped. "I'm free, Alex. What do you need?"

Alexandra had pushed a policeman away from his motorcycle, borrowed his ride, and followed the ambulance through traffic. She replied, "Maybe a real ambulance in case this doesn't go well."

"What's going on?"

Voltaic explained as Alexandra focused on the road.

Danica replied, "Then there's not much I can do. Get him, Alex."

"You know it."

The ambulance couldn't reach full speed in the thick traffic, although it had sirens. She was lucky the bad guys hadn't considered magical transport for themselves. As she swerved across three lanes to avoid a cab that had braked for no reason, she wondered why they hadn't killed him and run since they'd taken a shot at him. It seemed impossible that it could have been two unrelated attacks simultaneously in the same place.

None of that mattered at the moment. She needed to get the ambulance stopped, fast. Only one way to accomplish it without risking injury to Damien came to mind.

She pulled the motorcycle over to the driver's side and acted like she was about to surge forward. When the ambulance veered to smash into her, she pulled back and whipped around the opposite side. She fired her pistol at an angle into the passenger's window twice to break the glass.

As the ambulance veered right to slam into her, she jumped off the bike and onto the door. She snaked one arm inside and grabbed the handle, and the door swung free. Alexandra rode the momentum, spun, and got her foot on the running board when it stopped.

The person behind the wheel had a pistol, but she jumped inside and grabbed his hand as he brought it up. Her legs were still outside the vehicle as she tussled with him, and she yanked them in just in time to avoid a car.

The ambulance slewed from side to side as the driver fought for control, and she slammed the bottom of her fist down on the man's wrist. It snapped, and the gun fell free. She pulled herself up, slammed her foot down on the brake, and punched him in the face with one hand while she used the other to control the ambulance. Several more punches rendered him unable to fight her, and the ambulance stopped.

Police cars pulled up as she rushed into the back to check on Damien. He'd been strapped in and was in good shape. The medic who'd been with him hadn't been and was unconscious on the floor of the ambulance. She announced, "I have him. He's safe."

Danica replied, "Good work, partner. Jilly says so too."

Alexandra laughed and let out a long sigh as the adrenaline left her. "Thanks. I think I need a drink."

Danica laughed. "Sounds right to me. Drinks for everyone. We'll call that a new company ritual."

CHAPTER NINETEEN

Danica had taken the man she'd captured on the rooftop back to the warehouse and handed him over to Zack, then portaled back to New York City to retrieve Alexandra. They bounced to Miami so the other woman could change, then portaled to the warehouse.

Then Danica bounced home, changed into something more comfortable, and returned. She laughed as she considered that so far, her new job had involved a lot of transporting other people.

Zack was supervising robots constructing another room. "How's our guest?"

The tech shrugged. "I gave him some water a while ago. He's still tied up in there." He tapped his glasses. "We have an eye on him."

"Let's go have a conversation with the gentleman, shall we?"

"Let's. I need to grab some things first. Give me a second."

She and Alexandra walked toward the room where they had stored their captive.

Zack arrived a moment later with a metal chair and a handful of sensor pads. "We have the network up in here. Voltaic is testing it out for me, so she can give us a hand here while she does that."

Alexandra asked, "Is that the only chair?"

"I thought our guest should probably sit through this."

"And us?"

He smiled. "You're both strong, healthy, and athletic. I figured you could probably handle it."

Danica replied, "And tired." She looked at Alexandra. "Let's go grab some chairs."

A few moments later, everyone was in the room. The prisoner was duct-taped to a chair at arms and ankles, and Zack was finishing up placing sensors on his neck, wrists, and ankles. Danica sat normally in her chair while Alexandra had spun hers around and straddled it. Danica took a moment to assess their prisoner. She hadn't gotten a good look at him while they fought.

He had short hair that was messy on top but probably normally better kept. His face was rectangular with a hard jaw. His eyes showed weakness, a sort of scared softness that didn't fit with the rest of the look. He was on the thin side of muscular and built like a runner. He was clad in urban camouflage pants, military boots, and a gray T-shirt, all of which looked like they'd probably come from an Army Navy store after being heavily used by their original owners.

Zack moved away when he finished.

Danica nodded at their guest. "Hi, I'm Danica. I'd say

I'm sorry for scraping you over the gravel roof, but you did try to shoot me, so I figure at worst we're even."

He stared at her. "This is Alexandra. She dealt with your friends who tried to kidnap Damien Zane." Again, he didn't react. She sighed inwardly. "You've met Zack, and our info-mancer is on the line, acting as our lie detector."

Alexandra asked, "What's your name?"

He tilted his head. "John. John Doe. Maybe you've heard of me." There was a little spine in his response.

Danica asked, "Why shoot him?"

Their prisoner shrugged. "I hated him. His music sucks. The world would be better off without him." Danica could almost hear the unspoken, "Blah, blah, blah."

Voltaic's voice issued from Danica's phone. "That's a lie."

Alexandra laughed. "So, you're a fan?"

The man replied, "Hardly."

"So, which part was the lie? That you hated him or that his music is terrible?"

Danica replied, "Both, probably. I bet he's a fanboy."

Alexandra asked, "You hate him?"

"Yes."

Voltaic stated, "Lie."

Danica shook her head. "You're not being very friendly. Here we are, being nice to you, and you're giving us nothing."

He met her eyes and drawled, "I'm duct-taped to a chair. That's not exactly a move engineered to build rapport."

She shrugged. "You're not dead. You could be, you know. We're not police."

"Fine. I was hired." His demeanor changed as he spoke. His voice deepened, his eyes became clear and confident, and his spine straightened. His presence filled his half of the room.

Alexandra asked, "You're a pro?"

He nodded. "Yes. And this conversation is inadmissible. Any proof that I did it is gone."

Danica kept her face neutral but grumbled inwardly. Unfortunately, he was correct on all counts. "Who hired you?"

"Don't know and wouldn't tell you if I did. Like she said. I'm a professional."

Alexandra asked, "Who was the magical who was supporting you?" Danica had shared the whole story with her while they traveled.

He voiced a dark laugh. "An incompetent bastard."

"How were you hired?"

"You know how it goes. Message board, virtual chat room, untraceable payments. It's not hard to get someone knocked off these days. Even notable someones."

Danica asked, "Do you have any idea why someone wanted him dead?"

The man laughed. "Seriously. Have you heard his music?"

She rolled her eyes. "Besides that."

"Don't know, don't care. The money was right, with a bonus for success."

Danica frowned. "Wait. You were paid regardless of whether you succeeded and got a bonus if you did?" He nodded, and she looked at Alexandra. "Ever heard anything like that?"

The other woman shook her head. "Nope. How about you, V?"

The infomancer replied, "Nothing. Seems weird to me."

Danica asked, "What's your opinion, hired gun?"

The prisoner rolled his neck with his eyes closed before answering. "I asked myself that question. I figured maybe multiple teams competing. It's not unheard of, although it's rare. But if you really want the job done, you layer your attacks, just like you expect your opponents to layer their defenses."

Danica shook her head. "I don't like you." She stood and motioned to Zack. "Make sure he doesn't go anywhere."

While she and Alexandra walked out, she dialed Arthur and explained the situation. He agreed that his people could take charge of the captive. They knew some people who would probably be able to get any information he had so far been reluctant to share.

Danica shoved her phone into her pocket. "Okay. Let's go get that drink."

Forty-five minutes later, they were at a bar in Cleveland called Revels. It was moderately fancy in that it had one of those garage doors that opened to turn it into an indoor-outdoor restaurant and a bunch of chrome. On the other hand, there were no fancy drinks, only an impressive selection of draft beers and the usual cocktails.

Danica opted for a local draft, a Great Lakes Burning River Pale Ale, as did Alexandra, who chose an Edmund Fitzgerald Robust Porter. Zack ordered an Old Fashioned. Voltaic, who was present at their table through Danica's phone on its surface, commented, "I'm having a margarita in solidarity with you."

Alexandra laughed. "Right on, sister. Nice job today, by the way."

Voltaic replied, "And to all of you. Wasn't clean and smooth, but I don't see how we could've done better."

Danica remarked, "Unfortunately, we need to figure out how to do better. That chucklehead seems to have brought some serious heat down on himself."

"Well, his music is pretty annoying." Everyone laughed at the infomancer's comment.

Alexandra observed, "We need more people. And more gear."

Voltaic offered, "I have lots of schedule flexibility. I can help out whenever you need me, as long as I get a little advance notice."

Zack added, "I have the body armor fitting set up for tomorrow. My contact will almost certainly have some other stuff you'd like, too."

Danica nodded. "That leaves us still needing some warm bodies and with the urgent need to get Rockstar's people to do a better job of reining him in."

Alexandra asked, "Why would anyone hate him enough to go to this extent? Like, I could see one shooter. It's still a lot of effort, don't get me wrong, but I could see it. The backup team, though? That's a lot. Especially since, if what assassin boy had to say is correct, they paid the going rate and offered a bonus on top of it."

Danica replied, "I'm not sure the bullet was supposed to land. Although why put a high-quality individual behind the gun, then?" She shook her head. "I don't know. The only thing I do know is that we need to do better."

Zack countered, "Don't sell yourself short. You foiled

an assassination and a kidnapping. That's a lot for your first day."

Alexandra agreed. "He's not wrong."

Danica nodded. "I know. I just hope we're enough to save him from whoever's trying to kill him." Jilly made a small sound from inside her jacket, and she patted the tiny dragon's head where she nestled in her pocket. Among other things, Jilly thought they should go to sleep.

"A lot of day left," Zack commented.

Alexandra replied, "I'm going to spend it alternating hot showers and naps until tomorrow." They clinked glasses and agreed that was a good plan for all of them, and they'd earned it.

CHAPTER TWENTY

Danica awoke to a slight breeze on her face. She opened her eyes and saw Jilly sitting on her chest and staring at her. The tiny dragon had used her wings to create said breeze. She mumbled, "What?"

Jilly pointed out, "This is the time you normally get up. The ringing didn't happen, so I thought I'd help."

The dragon hopped off onto the pillow Danica normally hugged during the night as she sat up. "That's because I didn't need to be up so early today."

Jilly insisted, "But it's time."

Danica laughed and extended a finger to scratch the dragon under the chin. Jilly stretched her neck and accepted it. "All right then. I guess I'll get up."

"If you have time, we can go out for breakfast again."

Danica laughed as she threw the covers off. "Oh, now I see what this is all about."

The dragon flapped her wings and landed on Danica's shoulder. "Blueberries are delicious."

"We have blueberries in the fridge."

"Not blueberries and syrup." The way the dragon said the last word made it seem almost magical.

Danica shook her head but couldn't hide her grin. "It was a mistake taking you to IHOP."

Jilly flew a quick figure eight, clearly for the fun of it. "I want to try all the syrups."

"Of course you do. All right. Just let me shower and get dressed, okay?"

The dragon flew off to the living room, and Danica got to her morning routine. Half an hour later, she texted Alexandra and Zack to see if they wanted to come to breakfast. Both said they'd just gotten out of bed like normal people and declined. She headed to IHOP and enjoyed pancakes with all of their syrups, plus a healthy dose of eggs for the protein she'd need to keep her brain functioning through the day ahead.

When they finished, Jilly commented, "I like strawberry too. And raspberry."

"Of course you do."

"You should've stolen some of those packets of honey."

Danica laughed. "I can buy packets of honey. I don't need to steal them from the restaurant."

The dragon flapped around to look her in the eyes. "Do you have any right now?"

"No."

"Then you should've stolen some." The dragon shook her head as if Danica was too stupid to live and impossible to teach, then flew back to her shoulder.

At the agreed-upon time, Danica portaled Zack to the Spellbound office in Miami, then retrieved Alexandra. From there they grabbed a company SUV, and Zack drove them out to a large, four-story building done entirely in mirrored glass. The light shining off it made her squint and raise her hand against it. Jilly raised a wing on her shoulder, mimicking her.

Alexandra observed, "Damn, that's ostentatious."

Zack laughed. "They're a tech startup. They need to be fancy to get that sweet, sweet venture capital."

"How do you know them?"

"Helped out in the early days. Hold some stock."

Danica replied, "So, this is kind of reverse insider trading."

Zack countered, "You make no sense."

Danica sighed. She felt that way most of the time lately. "I know."

The lobby was impressive, as was the man standing behind the reception desk. His tight suit showed off his slenderness in a way that made him seem almost alien. Zack waved and took them straight to the back.

They located the owner in a large workspace, walking on a treadmill behind a computer. He stepped off and hugged Zack. When they broke the clinch, Zack introduced them. "Simon, this is Alexandra, Danica, and Jilly." The dragon waved.

Simon grinned. "Fantastic. Good to meet you all. Zack said you're looking for some body armor and some 'cool spy stuff.'"

Danica laughed. "I guess that's accurate."

"Well then, come with me." He took them through a different door into a short hallway, then through a sliding door into another cavernous space. This one was full of humming equipment and smelled like hot plastic, metal, and ammonia mixed with a slight scorch of electricity.

Simon explained, "The other space is for research. This is for fabrication." He reached into a cabinet and pulled out two items. He tossed one each to Alexandra and Danica. "These help the scanner. Please put them on." They both turned their backs and changed into the T-shirts.

Behind them, Zack added, "I'll need one too."

"They're letting you go out into the field? Do they even know you?" The sound of flesh striking flesh sounded, and Simon laughed. "Ow. That was uncalled for. Fine."

When Danica turned, Simon pointed at a cylindrical object about eight feet tall and three feet in diameter. "Go in there so we can scan you. I'm afraid you'll have to leave the dragon out here."

Danica moved toward the cylinder as Jilly lifted off her shoulder, flapped her wings, and landed on Alexandra's shoulder. When she stepped inside, the cylinder rotated closed. A soft light came on, and lasers ran over her body from every direction.

Simon's disembodied voice informed her, "The process takes forty-five seconds. Hopefully you're not claustrophobic."

She walked out after that interval and waited while the other two got their scans. When they finished, Simon pulled all three scans up to show the models of their torsos rendered in the computer. He asked, "What kind of protection do you need?"

Danica replied, "Bullets and blades, ideally."

He nodded and hit some buttons. "How heavy?"

Danica looked at Alexandra, who replied, "Let's say

medium. We need to be strong, but we also might be standing around in it for hours before any action happens, so it can't be too heavy."

Simon nodded and hit some more buttons. Then he looked over his shoulder. "What's your budget?"

Danica replied, "Whatever it needs to be. I'll find the money."

He laughed. "Now that's the kind of answer I like to hear. I have some new materials we've been working with that I can use." He hit some buttons, then turned away from the computer. "The items are in the queue. They'll be ready by tomorrow afternoon."

Danica frowned. "That long?"

He nodded. "It's a multilayer weave rather than ceramic plates, and it's all metal filament. It takes our printers a long time to do the weaves, one layer after the next after the next. In principle, it works the same as a car in a crash. The outer layers crumple to absorb the kinetic energy as they give way and there's enough of them to stop the bullet or the blade before it gets in."

Danica raised her hands. "You're talking to someone who can't even cook well, much less do science. I'll take your word for it."

Simon laughed again. She'd always imagined people involved in startups would be constantly stressed, but he didn't seem to have a care in the world. "Zack, I like your friends. What else do you need?"

Alexandra had been thinking about that. "Low-profile cameras that can access our comm system, with sticky pads. Sensors that can do the same."

Simon nodded and tapped his watch, which emitted a

hologram that rotated above his wrist. "Something like this?"

The devices were small, and Danica trusted they would do what Alexandra had asked for. "Perfect."

Alexandra added, "Locator tags that can use our comms or hijack cell phone networks and so forth. Lockpicks for electronic and physical locks."

Simon nodded. "Doable."

Zack interjected, "You all are thinking small. Grenades. Other explosives to open doors and such. Restraints. Tasers. Anti-magic frangible ammo."

Danica added, "Healing and energy potions."

Alexandra opened her mouth to speak, but Simon raised his hands and chuckled. "Okay. That's quite the shopping list for now. I'll get to it. You'll have all that tomorrow afternoon, too."

He took them into his office, where an espresso machine provided cups for all of them. They sat around a table in comfortable chairs and discussed other options. Alexandra said, "Knives, plus a multi-tool, would be good."

Danica nodded. "I hate to think we'll get into enough of a fight that knives will matter, but you're right. Better to have and not need and all that."

Zack rubbed his chin. "Not to get too James Bond here, but what about emergency tech? Something that can cut through restraints if something goes wrong, portable medkits, that kind of thing?"

Simon shrugged. "Yeah, I can't do much for you on that front, I'm afraid."

"I can do some looking around. If we can't find it, I can try to make it when I'm not working on other stuff."

Simon added, "He's good at it. I was sad to lose him."

Danica chuckled. "I figured he annoyed you so much that you fired him."

Zack rolled his eyes. "You see? No respect, anywhere. I left because Simon's a control freak."

The other man laughed. "He's right. He did. I am. I'm not proud of it, but I can't seem to change it, either." They chatted for a few more minutes about the history between Simon and Zack, then Danica looked at her watch and released a long, heartfelt groan.

Simon asked, "Something wrong?"

She nodded. "Arthur and I have to go meet with the rock star."

Alexandra asked, "The man himself?"

She nodded. "Yeah."

Zack laughed. "You have fun with that. Sometimes it's good not to be the boss."

CHAPTER TWENTY-ONE

After a quick conversation with Arthur, Danica turned the tables on her partners and dragged Alexandra and Zack to the meeting with Damien Zane. As they entered the lobby of his hotel in New York City, she murmured, "A guard near the elevator."

Alexandra replied, "Another, undercover, in the café."

Zack added, "Maybe one off to the right. Although he might just be admiring Arthur's suit."

Arthur turned to look. "I appreciate his good taste." They all laughed softly.

The guard by the elevator nodded at them as they pressed the button, and Arthur returned the gesture. Danica felt confident about the first-floor security, anyway. The protectors had eyes on the elevators and staircases and were doubtless in contact with someone in the office with the camera feeds.

They rode up in silence, then stepped out into the hallway when the door opened. Security people stood on either side of the elevator, and another was by the door to Damien's suite.

Danica observed, "Not bad, but I don't sense any magic. They should have someone on the team to defend against a magical incursion or be running a lot of anti-magic emitters."

Arthur replied, "Unfortunately, people with the right set of talents for this gig who also possess magic aren't all that plentiful."

"You're saying I should have asked for more money."

Arthur laughed. "No, you definitely shouldn't have."

Zack whispered, "I think that means yes."

Danica replied, "Yeah, I figured that out. Thanks, man."

Jilly laughed from her inner pocket.

The guard opened the door to the suite, and they stepped inside. The living room was huge, and the back wall was full of windows that looked out over the New York City skyline. Danica recognized one of his assistants when she came over and offered them coffee or soda. Arthur took the former. The rest of them took sodas.

They sat on the couches and had their drinks in hand when Damien and the other assistant Danica recognized walked in, along with a man in a suit she hadn't yet met. Rockstar grumbled, "They won't let me go back to my house. Tell me it's your fault."

Arthur calmly replied, "Someone did try to kill you or abduct you, so some precautions are necessary."

"Yeah. What was up with that? Confused bad guys? And which one of you knocked me down?"

Danica replied, "We're not sure yet. And I did that."

He made a sound like a harrumph and sat. "Thanks for that."

She couldn't tell if he was being sarcastic or sincere. One of his assistants handed him a mug of coffee, then broke open an airplane bottle of bourbon and poured it into the mug.

Damien winced as he took a long drink, sighed, and leaned back on the couch. "Michael, introduce yourself."

The suited man standing by the couch during the interaction smiled faintly. "I'm Michael Prescott. Chief of Damien's security."

Arthur replied, "Pleased to meet you." He rose and shook the man's hand.

Alexandra asked, "What's the plan in the near term? Hole up here?"

Prescott answered, "No, unfortunately. We have three days of rehearsals to get everything down before the stage needs to be moved to the venue for the warmup shows."

Arthur asked, "Is the rehearsal location secret?"

Prescott responded with a sharp nod. "We've done our best to keep it so. We've labeled the trucks as something else. There's no tour bus and so forth. But people still work there, and they'll know what's going on. It might not be easily accessible information, but it's out there somewhere."

Zack suggested, "We could ask our infomancer to keep an eye on some keywords related to the show and the venue. See if anyone's talking."

Prescott nodded. "Good plan. We have ours doing the same, but it can't hurt."

Danica asked, "Why isn't there a magical on your security team?"

"We have several. The one on duty right now is downstairs conferring with the one who works for the hotel. The suite is equipped with an automatic anti-magic emitter. It senses magic, and it goes active. Portaling in here would be bad, I'm told."

"Why not have it on all the time?"

"You'd have to ask the hotel, but I presume it's because some people choose to disable it. It's optional. We have it turned on, of course."

Danica had the sudden urge to cast a spell to see what would happen. Arthur bumped her arm as if he knew what she was thinking, and she let the desire dissipate.

The conversation about security measures continued, then suddenly Damien interrupted and demanded, "Did you figure out who's behind it?" Even Prescott looked shocked by the sudden outburst.

Danica shook her head. "No, not yet."

He surged up and pointed at each of them in turn as he shouted, "You're investigators, aren't you? Investigate." He stomped out of the room.

Silence reigned, then Prescott commented, "He's still a little wound up. It's not every day you're forced to acknowledge that not everyone loves you. Especially when adulation is your drug of choice."

The song *Love is the Drug* by Bryan Ferry passed through Danica's mind.

Arthur mildly replied, "Technically, we're not investigators."

"We know. *He* knows. He's like this. He'll be better later.

He won't be sorry or anything, but he won't carry a grudge. Never does. And never really understands why other people do."

Danica nodded. "It's understandable that he's a little rattled. What are you doing for security at the venue?"

"We'll focus on perimeter security during the rehearsals. We're using magical transport in and out of the venue for him and the band. Everyone else will need a pass and will be checked for the usual stuff."

"And during the shows?"

"We're still working that out. Each venue is different, so we have to adapt to all of them. They all have security people too, with their own personalities. It's a constant act of negotiation."

Zack muttered, "It's a bad situation."

Danica asked, "How will he be transported from city to city during the tour?"

"He has a private plane."

One of the assistants interjected, "He likes taking fans with him on the plane."

Danica scowled. "He's not using it. Magical transport only until we have this figured out."

Prescott countered, "He won't like that."

"If you won't listen to our advice, we can walk. This is what you're paying us for." She glanced at Arthur, who nodded.

Prescott looked as if his stomach was bothering him. "Okay. I'll work on him. Consider it a done deal unless I tell you it's not."

They discussed specifics for another twenty minutes, then took their leave. When they were out on the street,

Alexandra began to speak, but Arthur raised a hand. "Hold on. Danica, can you take us back to my office?"

She opened a portal, and Arthur waved them all to seats as he dropped into the one behind his desk. "This space is secure from eavesdropping. I think from now on, we should keep communications as secure as possible."

Zack frowned. "Something in particular you're worried about?"

Arthur ran a hand through his hair, one of the only signs of stress he ever exhibited to Danica's knowledge. "No. Just that anyone who's after him now knows additional security is in place and might have a line on who we are. If they do, they might feel the need to take proactive steps to compromise that security."

Zack asked, "Are you saying we're in danger?"

Arthur shook his head. "Not as long as you're smart. Stay alert, though. Magical transport when it makes sense, keep an eye on your surroundings, that sort of thing."

Danica interjected, "Rockstar made one good point. I think we need to get proactive. Secure some investigative talent and put them to work."

"I fully agree. Let me work on that while you all check out the rehearsal."

CHAPTER TWENTY-TWO

A magical from Prescott's team met them at the hotel and portaled them to the venue at the agreed-upon time. From the outside, it looked like another large warehouse with nothing special about it aside from a serious power supply as evidenced by heavy lines at a junction nearby. As Prescott had claimed, the trailer trucks were entirely nondescript, and a construction trailer appeared to be the band's temporary home instead of something obvious like a tour bus.

Danica commented, "So far, so good."

Alexandra replied, "Yeah, you can't even tell the sheer amount of ego contained in the space. Amazing."

Zack laughed as he slipped on his glasses. "I'll take a walk around the perimeter so Voltaic can get a good look. We'll want to bring a pair of drones and a charging station here before we leave today."

Alexandra asked, "We have those?"

Zack replied, "Voltaic has those. They're on loan."

Danica frowned suspiciously. "Was Voltaic part of your startup too? Or do you get a kickback?"

"I've been around. I know people. I'm loyal. So sue me."

Alexandra commented, "Bold thing to say to people with pistols."

He lifted his hand, made it look like it was talking, and turned away.

Danica couldn't make out his words as he spoke to Voltaic on a private channel and figured that was for the best. "All right, let's head inside."

They entered from backstage through a small door set in the middle of the building, then had to walk half the length of the stage to get out to the side of it and into the open area. Equipment was arranged in racks on the stage and in the audience area. Lights hung from heavy black trusses mounted above the stage and about a third of the way deep into the space. They supported several cylinders and boxes that made no sense to Danica. Huge speaker arrangements hung from the ceiling.

The magical who had brought them explained, "This isn't quite perfect for rehearsals because venues always have a grid of girders to hook up to and this place doesn't. But it's close enough, and the building's structural integrity is up to the weight."

Danica replied, "One more reason people might not look for Zane here. All to the good." As they came out in front of the stage, she saw a riser for the drums, lower risers for each guitarist, and a microphone stand placed in the center. The backdrop was a huge video screen, far bigger than any she'd ever seen, that occupied the entire width of the stage and went up as high as the lighting grid. "Wow."

Their escort laughed. "Yeah, Damien does it up big. Pyro, video, lights, sounds, all of it. I have to get back to the hotel. If you need anything, just grab someone in a crew shirt." There were a ton of them around, bustling from place to place and seemingly working quite hard. She and Alexandra found a couple of folding chairs and a rolling storage unit and set them down in front of the stage, to one side of the extension that ran out into the crowd.

Danica remarked, "I don't like the look of that runway."

Alexandra replied, "Agreed."

Voltaic announced her presence by saying, "You'll hate it even more once you see this. Glasses on?"

Danica replied, "Just a sec." She fished hers out from an inner pocket and put them on. Alexandra did the same. A point-of-view virtual reality representation of a Damien Zane concert completely blocked their view of the auditorium. Rockstar skipped down the runway playing his guitar, then stopped while the band did solos to slap hands with people.

Danica muttered, "It looks like he's going to…"

Alexandra finished, "Jump in the crowd," as he did exactly that.

They swarmed him, giving him hugs, high-fives, and so forth. Large security personnel pried fans away so he could return to the stage after about a minute.

Alexandra grumbled, "This is going to suck."

Danica replied, "I can shield him if I need to. It's not an absolute disaster."

Voltaic laughed. "Only a partial one."

A bustle of activity around the stage caught their attention, and they watched as technicians melted away from view. Then the band arrived, laughing and joking together as they walked in.

Damien waved at them with a smile, and they waved back. He seemed completely unlike the person they met earlier, as if real life was anxiety-inducing for him but this was his happy place. Again, Danica imagined that the kind of adulation one got as a celebrity would quickly become addictive.

A man in a crew shirt jogged out to them and introduced himself. "Seth Jasik, I'm the stage manager. This is a first run-through, so I can watch from out here with you. They'll spend ten minutes or so tuning. Are there any questions I can answer?"

Alexandra beat Danica to the question. "Does he have to go into the crowd?"

Jasik laughed. "Yes. It's expected. They would stampede if he didn't do it. Fans are like that. Once you do a thing, it's canon, and changing it is asking for trouble."

Alexandra offered, "Not the safest choice."

"It's been my experience that safety is not the first thing on Damien's mind."

Danica laughed. "Yeah, we're definitely getting that impression too."

Video started to play on the back wall, and loud music screamed out of the speakers with only a moment's static as a warning. Danica set up a sound shield around Jilly to protect her ears.

The noise killed their conversation. Their earpieces easily brought the noise down to a useful level and could still filter for conversation, but the ones the stage manager wore weren't quite as advanced. She would have shielded him too, but figured he probably needed to hear.

They watched the first three songs. Then someone called a halt to reset and try them again. Jasik ran forward to get involved as the band got together to talk with the technicians at the side of the stage, and Michael Prescott wandered up to join them.

Danica commented, "This place is nicely anonymous like you said. I doubt we'll have any problems here. What's the security plan during the warmup shows?"

"Venue security handles the outside. We don't have a piece of that, although we'll keep an eye on it. A secondary unit of my people will be on constant guard around the tour buses and trucks, even though those are technically within the purview of venue security. The primary unit will handle backstage in the venue and control of the area around the stage on the floor. Venue security watches the rest of the inside."

"Seems like a challenge for everyone involved."

"It is. The venue has standard detectors at the entrances to find weapons, explosives, and that type of thing. We'll have them in the back too, and every entrance in our area will have one of our people present to check IDs. We have a tiered pass system, and there will be sensors on doorways between sections to ensure that only those who have the appropriate pass can get through."

Alexandra interjected, "We'll need those."

Prescott nodded. "You'll have them. Also, we'll have anti-magic emitters covering the place. They'll be suspended from the grid so no one can mess with them.

They're ours, so we don't need to depend on venue equipment for that."

Danica remarked, "I'm not against the idea. But why is it necessary?"

He offered a thin smile. "You only have to learn once that magic and pyrotechnics don't work together to ensure it doesn't happen again."

Alexandra laughed. "That's a story I have to hear."

He shrugged. "It wasn't us, but back in the early days, a magical in the crowd decided to do some of their own pyrotechnics. That would've been mostly harmless, I guess, but something they did triggered the pyrotechnics behind the stage. One of the artists was close by and almost took a firework in the face. Fortunately, he dodged, and the band played it off for laughs. But the lesson was learned."

The band started playing again, and they walked farther back into the venue to continue talking. Damien ran down the runway, and Danica asked again, "Does he have to work the crowd like that?"

Prescott shrugged. "He won't be stopped."

"How about a shield? No, anti-magic, right. Could we get him to wear body armor?"

A laugh escaped Prescott, loud enough to echo a little in the back of the warehouse. "He's mostly shirtless for half the show, so no."

Alexandra added, "Fans expect it."

"They do."

Danica shook her head. "How long would it delay the tour if I blew up that huge video screen?"

Prescott laughed again. "Not long enough to make it

worthwhile. Plus, the insurance people would probably bankrupt your whole company."

"Damn."

They watched for thirty minutes as the band worked through several of their biggest hits. Then they paused, and Damien bounded down from the stage and came over to them. He was all smiles as he asked, "What did you think?"

Alexandra replied, "Sounds amazing."

Danica nodded in agreement.

"Hopefully the fans will dig it. We've only announced the first leg of the tour, but if it goes well, we've got much bigger plans all around the world." A band member shouted, and he hustled off.

Danica and Alexandra looked at each other and groaned. Danica stated, "We need to find the source of the threat. I can't deal with this guy for the duration of those bigger plans."

Alexandra replied, "Yeah, screw this reactionary stuff. Time to get proactive."

"I couldn't agree more."

CHAPTER TWENTY-THREE

The virtual space was the same as the previous times Madden Wells had met with the representative. That was how he knew him, no name, just "the representative." He had hired an infomancer to coordinate with the other man's—presumably a man, although in this space, no one could be sure—infomancer to set up this neutral ground. The space was modeled after a hotel lobby and simulated people bustled around, doing their simulated things.

The ground was the only neutral thing about the meeting. Their relationship was anything but since he was a tiny fish in this dramatically dangerous ocean. His avatar looked nothing like himself. It had a bland, generic face and a squared-off body like something from a twentieth-century game. He'd chosen it as a mark of his displeasure about this arrangement, but he was certain the man he was meeting didn't care.

Wells sat at the bar that ran along one side of the space. The bartender approached, but a wave sent him away. A moment later, the representative sat beside him.

He turned and saw that he looked like he had on previous occasions. A tall, thin man wearing a blue pinstripe suit, white shirt, and purple tie. His belt and shoes were brown and shone like they were brand new. His black hair was perfectly coiffed and pulled back from his face in neat and orderly rows, his part so straight it might have been done with a ruler.

Wells nodded a greeting. "Thanks for coming."

The other man inclined his head. "Of course. We like to keep our clients happy."

Wells cut in, "What was that debacle, then? Because I can assure you, I'm not happy. Not happy that it failed, and not happy that it came as a surprise to me."

The representative shrugged. His voice maintained an infuriating neutrality. "A test run. If it had worked, that would've been lovely, but we never counted on it doing so. It's notable that it would have succeeded if not for the undercover security we weren't aware of. Now that we know they're in play, we'll adapt accordingly."

Wells fought down the urge to yell. It wouldn't accomplish anything in the real world, and his avatar was set not to show emotion, so it wouldn't do anything in the simulation, either. "Why did you try to kill him? I didn't ask for that. In fact, I specified that I want him alive." A bullet would end Zane's pain too quickly.

The representative waved a hand as if pushing the notion aside. "We didn't try to kill him. The shooter had orders to miss and was intended to cause chaos. The shot opened the door for the medics to make their play."

He wanted to argue. Wanted to explain how stupid that

was. That, too, would accomplish nothing. "Now I hear the shooter's been captured."

"True. He won't give anything away and they won't have any evidence to hold him on. That's why we went with a professional, to ensure no blowback was possible that might endanger accomplishing our goal."

Wells snorted. "You're assuming the other side plays by the rules."

The representative tapped a finger on the bar to emphasize his words. "I'm assuming nothing of the sort. We used magic to wipe the details from his brain, including all conscious knowledge that he was supposed to miss."

"That's an alarming thing to do."

A small smile appeared on the representative's face. "Alarming for those who stand against us. For those who seek out our services, much less so. As I said, that's why we went with a professional, because he understood the necessity."

Wells forced his brain back onto productive topics. "All right. I understand. I apologize for my doubts. This is just so...personal." He steadied himself. "What's the plan now?"

"Largely the same. We'll identify several possibilities for extracting him from his protection and bring him to you. We'll chain them, either enacted simultaneously on the same night or several if needed."

Wells grumbled, "This is costing me a fortune."

The representative countered, "You agreed to that upfront."

He nodded his avatar's emotionless head. "Yes. I did.

But maybe there should be a penalty for failure rather than a bonus for success, given the current trend."

The representative laughed, and there was condescension in the sound. "Only if you want exclusively third-rate talent."

Wells countered, "Is that not what we had for the first attempt? I don't seem to have Damien Zane on his knees begging for his life, as I was promised."

"Not yet, but you will."

Wells retorted, "I have doubts," and immediately wished he could take it back.

The other man raised an eyebrow. His avatar made the gesture seem entirely natural. "Would you like me to share your concerns with *him?*"

Wells paled and applauded his earlier decision not to have his avatar convey emotion. "No. That's not necessary. I trust him implicitly, of course."

The other man's lips twitched up in a smile. "Of course. Is there anything else?" After Wells shook his head, the representative added, "Very well. You know how to reach me if there's a need." He disappeared from the simulation, and a moment later the simulation evaporated as well.

In the real world, Wells took off his VR goggles and the bracelets that tracked his hand motions. The room around him comforted him, as it always did. Glass cases filled with awards were placed all around the space, with more accolades hanging on the walls in frames. He turned to his assistant, who'd been sitting on the opposite side of his desk watching the interaction on a tablet. "Your assessment?"

The other man shrugged and adjusted his old-style

round glasses. "All seems to be progressing as well as it can, sir. I'm not sure there's much more we can do."

Wells squeezed his forehead in an attempt to lessen his headache. "You're right, I'm sure. It's just... Never mind."

"I understand the timetable is not to your liking. But your contractor comes highly recommended, as I understand it."

"The best in the business, that's what I hear from everyone. Mysterious as hell, but very good at what he does." He waved irritably. "Presumably a he. Who the hell knows when it's all virtual? It might be a cat."

The other man chuckled. "Then it would probably be wise to trust in him."

"You're right, you're right. Go away. Go do work. Leave me to fret."

His assistant stood. "Are you sure?"

"Positive. Go." When he was alone in the room, Wells rose from his chair with a groan. The extra pounds he carried made even the smallest thing difficult.

He headed for the small bar cart in the corner, mixed a gin and tonic, and ambled around the room. It was done up in dark green paint with a chair rail at waist height and expensive mahogany paneling below it. Comfortable chairs were in various places with small tables beside them. The carpet underneath was expensive and comfortable to walk on.

Cases held Grammy awards, Emmy awards, and Oscars, all for albums or soundtracks his record label had produced. The record label had Damien Zane locked into a contract that had him over a barrel. Then somehow he'd wriggled out.

One day, he declared he was no longer working for the company. When they went to Legal to get copies of the contracts, they were gone. The physical copies, gone. The electronic copies, gone. Wells couldn't imagine how that had happened. It was impossible, everyone told him. Yet it was true.

Zane's next album had started his meteoric rise. Every time Wells saw him on the screen, heard him on the radio, on an audio feed, or in a soundtrack, it was like a volcano burning inside. The gold and platinum records on the wall didn't assuage that pain. The other awards for him as one of the moguls of the music industry didn't quench it. Nothing did. The only thing that would work was revenge.

Several song lyrics touching on that subject flitted through his mind. Each made him feel better about what he was doing like it was a righteous response to what Damien thrice-damned Zane had done to him.

He sipped his drink as he stared absently across the room. Yes, there would be a reckoning once he had Zane in this room. He would offer to allow the prodigal son to return to the company and rejoin the label.

If he were smart, he would take that offer. If he was stupid, a musician's career could be ruined in oh so many ways. Everything from damaged vocal cords and hands to being locked up in a hospital for substance abuse issues or mental challenges, to being dropped into the World In Between and never heard from again.

Wells rather liked the second option best since having him committed as a lunatic would be the most humiliating end for Zane. When the moment came, he would go as instinct demanded. He always had, and it had brought him all these awards and enough wealth for his family to live comfortably for generations after he was gone, assuming he chose to give it to the ungrateful bastards.

He sat behind his desk and set the glass on a mahogany coaster that matched the paneling. He leaned back in his chair and closed his eyes with a broad smile as he once again imagined what it would be like to have Zane on his knees begging for another chance.

CHAPTER TWENTY-FOUR

The next morning, Danica put on a dark suit with a cream blouse, some low-heeled but stylish boots, and a few pieces of jewelry. She was trying to make a good impression, or the best one she could, anyway.

Jilly jumped on her shoulder, then crawled into her inside jacket pocket and curled up. It was impressive how big the tiny dragon could look when she was out with her wings spread compared to the small package she folded into in a pocket.

Danica wondered if there might be magic involved there, too. She didn't have much experience with creatures who were purely magic like Jilly. She gently patted her friend, then opened a portal and stepped through to the lobby of Spellbound's Miami office.

Arthur came out a moment later and smiled. As they climbed into the SUV, she asked, "Are we headed to the FBI office?" He'd explained that their potential investigator hire, Derek Reeves, was an FBI agent.

Arthur kept his eyes on the road. "Nope. Not sure if he doesn't want an apparent conflict of interest by having this conversation on FBI property or if he's just really busy. He told me he could give us fifteen minutes at the gun range."

Danica chuckled. "Do I have to beat him or something? Is this like when I met Alexandra?"

"Hopefully not. We don't want to damage his ego or anything."

"You're too kind."

He glanced at her with a grin. "Plus, it would be embarrassing if you lost."

She stuck her tongue out at him. "I take it back. And you're a jerk."

Arthur laughed. As they waited at a red light, he asked, "Do you think we have Rockstar under control?"

Danica snorted. "No one has Rockstar under control. That guy's a chucklehead."

"Well, I don't suppose I can argue with that. Are you satisfied with the safety arrangements for him?"

"I see a lot of danger points, and I wish I saw fewer. We've worked out plans for each of them. Still, the best solution is undoubtedly finding out who's after him and why, then finding them and making them stop. Either nicely or not-so-nicely."

Arthur nodded as he put the car back into motion. "Agreed. Always better to play offense when you can."

"Says someone whose company focuses on defense."

"Without offense, how could there be defense?"

Danica shook her head. "Sometimes I think you say stupid things just to irritate me."

He grinned at her again. "Only sometimes? I'm losing my touch."

They pulled up to a strip mall, where the anchor store at one end was a public shooting range. They went inside and donned ear protection, then stood and watched the people shooting. A half-dozen were present, but it was easy to pick out Derek from the description she'd received. Mid-thirties, tall and muscular, with neat brown hair and a "Superman jaw." The small scar on his left cheek was the clincher.

He was firing single shots, drawing from the hip, bringing the gun up, and firing in a smooth motion, then resetting and doing it again. When he emptied his magazine, he set the gun down, grabbed two empty mags from the small tray beside him, and brought all of them back to the counter. He refilled them, paid for the ammunition, and walked over to greet them with an outstretched hand. "Hello, Arthur."

Arthur shook it. "Good to see you, Derek. This is Danica."

The other man shifted his hand to her for a solid shake. "Pleasure to meet you. Any friend of Arthur's and all that."

Danica grinned. "You're friends with him voluntarily? I'm kind of stuck with him, longtime family friend." She rolled her eyes. "You can imagine."

Arthur shook his head. "The youth of today. Shall we head out and talk?"

Derek replied, "Let's." He led them to a coffee shop farther down the strip, bought them iced coffees, and got the same for himself. They sat at an outside table under an umbrella, and he exhaled a satisfied sigh. "No day is as good as the one that starts at the shooting range."

Danica asked, "Did you get all the bad guys?"

"All my rounds went more or less where they were supposed to go. Really, you know if it's gonna work after the first shot, but the rest is good practice."

"Have you ever used your weapon in the line of duty?"

He nodded. "But only as a threat. I had a bead on the guy and was locked in, but he let his hostage go and surrendered, so I didn't have to pull the trigger."

"Stressful moment."

Derek shrugged. "Yeah, but that's the job. Had some nightmares, talked to a Bureau therapist. It's all good. What can I do for you?"

Arthur explained, "We're staffing a Spellbound Security office in Cleveland. It's come to our attention while working our current case that we would benefit from someone with investigative experience. Danica has some training in the area but can't be everywhere at once. Adding another person with strong investigative skills would be a good idea. Naturally, I thought of you."

Derek nodded. "Always good to have people who can find answers to questions hanging around. What kind of cases do you have?"

Danica replied, "First client, actually. Damien Zane. We call him Rockstar. Have you heard of him?"

Derek laughed. "Who hasn't? He's like a megastar."

"He's a mega chucklehead."

Arthur laughed. "Don't insult our clients, Danica. That's not a positive step toward profitability."

Danica flicked her fingers as if shooing the comment

away. "He's not here to hear it, so I'll speak truth. Anyway, some bad people are after him, and it occurred to us that it might be nice to know who was behind the attack and the threats. Thus, the idea that having a sharp investigator-type person in the office would help."

Derek replied, "Makes sense. What's the situation now?"

"He was doing a concert for TV. Sniper shot at him from a window and missed. Our boy ran backstage into the arms of security like he should have, and an ambulance pulled up with medics ready."

Derek winced. "The medics were a snatch team, is that it?"

Arthur interjected, "See, I told you he was good."

Danica nodded. "Exactly right. We stopped them and also interrogated the shooter."

Derek continued. "You captured one, nice. Can I see the transcript?"

Danica called it up on her phone and handed it over. He flicked through it quickly, like he was a speed reader. "Bonus for success? That sounds like some kind of competition to me. That's our lead."

"It stood out to us too."

"Can we get more out of the source?"

Arthur shook his head. "No. Our docs say he's had his memory wiped."

Derek sniffed. "Magic, good and bad, like all things, down to the person using it."

From inside Danica's jacket came a muffled, "Good."

Derek raised an eyebrow. "Are you packing a concealed weapon?"

Danica laughed. "That's Jilly. She's a dragon. A very small, beautiful dragon. Who's mostly napping at the moment. She does a lot of that." An exaggerated snore emerged from her pocket.

Derek broke into a wide grin. "I look forward to meeting her."

"Take the job, and you can see her every day."

Arthur asked, "If you were part of the team, what would you do with the information we have?"

"Deals of that nature ordinarily take place in the virtual. I'm sure there's a place on the dark web where this sort of thing is discussed. Do you have an infomancer?"

She raised a hand and waggled it from side to side. "We have someone we can use on a freelance basis. Not a permanent team member yet."

Derek sipped his iced coffee. "Makes sense. Early days still, boots on the ground are probably more important to arrange first. If you decide to have your infomancer pursue that angle, let me know what you find. Maybe I can offer some insights."

Danica nodded. "Will do." They made small talk for a few minutes, then went their separate ways. Once they were back in the car, she observed, "I think we've got him."

Arthur nodded. "He'll need to think about it some. That's how he works. You should clear an office for him. I think he likes it where he is, but the variety of work you'll give him to do will tip the scales. Boredom is the mind-killer."

"Hopefully they tip quickly. We could use the help. And knock it off with the old movie references. It doesn't make you seem hip."

He laughed. "Are you going to take his advice on moving forward?"

"Absolutely. As soon as I leave you, I'll get in touch with Voltaic. Her bill's going to be high this month."

"Protect Zane, and we'll have enough money to pay her."

CHAPTER TWENTY-FIVE

Voltaic was in the zone, near the end of a first-person multiplayer shooter video game. The scenario she was streaming was team-based, and her team consisted of fans of her channel, which went by her gamer handle, Voltaic. Despite using the same name for her infomancy work, she could generally keep that part of her life away from the streaming fans.

A small window in the corner of her screen showed her avatar speaking over the view from the video game. Her hands flew over the keyboard, and she stomped on a custom device under her desk. She had wired guitar pedals to replicate some keys on the keyboard. Nothing inappropriate, only the control, the shift, the alt. Things where she'd be doing combo keys with her fingers, so she could use her feet instead of her hands and allow them to do other stuff.

Her character was a space marine dressed in power armor and wielding a pair of formidable pistols. It didn't have a helmet, so her avatar's head also showed. She narrated her strategy as she snuck along a girder at the top of a troop supply building and positioned herself over the defenders. They were in a rough outward-facing circle around the flag her team had to capture. She called for a distraction, and her teammates fired through the walls.

She dropped into the center of the circle and pulled the triggers of her twin custom pistols convulsively to shoot the defenders in the back. When the final enemy went down, the victory song played. Voltaic threw up her hands and crooned, "And that's how it's done. Thank you all for being here with me tonight, those in the game and everyone watching. I will see you all tomorrow night, same time, same place, for some sword and shield butchery."

Voltaic killed the stream and leaned back in her expensive gaming chair, which shifted and pulsed as it automatically moved into the best shape to support her reclining body. She was dressed in the same outfit her avatar wore because the streaming avatar was real-time video of her run through filters to protect her identity.

Her shirt had sponsor logos and fit tightly from wrist to neck and down to her waist, like a competitive cyclist might wear. She wore similarly styled leggings, even though they weren't seen, with more sponsor logos.

Voltaic checked to ensure her camera was off and her stream was dead, then stood and peeled off her shirt as she headed to her bedroom. She returned a few minutes later in a tank top and running shorts. Her long red hair was in a ponytail to keep it out of her face, and her many tattoos were visible on the bare skin of her arms, chest, and legs.

She popped the top off the bottle in her hand. Normally, she finished her stream and had a hard cider to wind down. Tonight it was an energy drink because she had work to do.

Frankly, Voltaic preferred it this way. She loved her work and doing it until she was exhausted was the best way to unwind, relax, and sleep. She dropped into her chair and hit some buttons to launch the programs she used for her infomancy work.

The energy hit her system as she reached out with her magic and interfaced with her ultra-high-powered computer system, which was faster than her gaming rig. A moment later she no longer saw the real world. Instead, she was inside the simulation. A single data point in the massive array of information that was the magical dark web.

Voltaic's starting point was always the same, a location she had crafted as her arming space and only she had access to. Theoretically someone else could find it, but it was well-hidden, and it wasn't like they could steal the programs the items on the shelves represented. Her avatar materialized inside it and was greeted by a British-accented robot voice. "Well, hello, Madame. You're back."

She replied, "Hello, Rust Bucket."

"I told you, my name is Oswald."

"Not to me." The robot was humanoid, but its features were too stiff to be taken as human. At best, it was an uncanny likeness. At worst it was downright spooky. "What do you have today?"

It was a silly question. The shop always had the same things, the virtual representations of the attack, defense, and utility programs she had loaded into her system. The place had a cluttered type of cyberpunk vibe. Neon signs on the walls promoted various brands, floor-to-ceiling shelves were full of equipment, and a worn wooden floor lay underfoot. A single door exited the space.

Oswald stood behind the counter with additional items on racks behind him. "What would you like today?"

"I don't know. Let me look around."

Her avatar had the same shade of red hair as hers, but it was styled up into almost a pompadour with the sides shaved. She wore a bodysuit similar to her streaming outfit but made of much stronger material with embedded armor plates to protect vital spots. Her boots were black, as were the calves of the suit, then it transitioned into yellow until it was finally orange and red at her neck and wrists. Someone had pointed out once that this look was more volcanic than voltaic, but she told him to bite her because she liked it the way it was.

An equipment belt lay around her hips and automatically adapted to whatever it needed to be as she added equipment. She went down the line of guns first. Many options were available, but the one she preferred was a blaster pistol similar to Han Solo's in *Star Wars*. She took it off the shelf, spun it, and moved it toward her thigh, where it slid into a holster that materialized to receive it.

Next up, she grabbed several explosive bricks and stuck them to her belt. After that, grenades of various types. Then knives that went on her upper arms, positioned hilt down for easy grabbing. All of that was standard, what she would wear for nothing more sinister than a night of conversation in a chat room.

Voltaic paused to consider what might lie ahead. It was doubtful she'd get into a serious fight, but she might be required to prove herself and should equip accordingly.

She added her wrist dart launchers, thick metal bracelets that could fire several different kinds of darts and were loaded with some of each type. Finally, she grabbed a grapnel launcher and secured it to her belt. She'd be in unknown territory, and a quick way out was always worth having.

Voltaic clapped her hands and rubbed them together. "I think I'm good. Put it on my tab."

Oswald sighed dramatically. "I believe I will rust away before you pay your tab, Madame."

Voltaic laughed, waved to open the door to leave, and dove out into the sky of the dark web. The landscape was like something out of a cyberpunk movie, maybe *Blade Runner*, and glittered below her as she fell. Vehicles flew through the air below her at various altitudes and speeds, and the ground was invisible through the thick mist that covered it.

She fired off searches on the dark web as she plummeted, looking for the most likely place where someone who wanted to contract killers and kidnappers might do that work. A number of possibilities came up, but as her systems did more of their work, one name recurred far more often than others. She angled in the proper direction and spread her arms wide at the appropriate moment.

Orange and black wings extruded to connect her wrists to her suit and reduce her speed. She adjusted her vector to avoid other pedestrians and landed in the street. She hit with her feet, rolled on her shoulder, and came up walking like nothing unusual had happened. A few people stared at her, and she stared a challenge back. No one accosted her.

Voltaic walked for several blocks until she found the place she wanted. It was on the ground floor of a tall building, and the only sign of its presence was a large fishhook that blinked in neon orange. She knew the place. Every infomancer who worked the line between legal and illegal knew it. It was Dive.

A keypad denied her entrance, but she launched a program that quickly cracked the code and opened it. It was a simple test to keep the lowest of the low out.

The door closed automatically behind her as she stepped inside. The interior was almost elegant in a strangely cartoonish kind of way. Display screens were mounted flush to the wall all over the place showing underwater scenes, each shaped like an oval as if it was a window to the outside.

Red tables sat between red vinyl booths, and every piece of wood held a nautical feature. An anchor here, a ship in a bottle there, large oars on the ceiling fan that circled lazily overhead. She'd always thought it a bit on the nose, but if you were going to have a theme, you might as well lean into it, right?

She swept her gaze around the room as she headed toward the bar. Each person she looked at immediately received a halo of data in her augmented vision, showing everything her systems could pull on those avatars. In general, people in here didn't look like they did in the real world, but most maintained a uniform image. It was possible to appear to be someone different every time you came in, but then you'd have no history to draw upon, no way to prove you were a regular.

Everyone in the room had an unsavory edge. Some were thieves, some blackmailers, and a few were peddlers in viruses and malware. Her falsified records would make her fit right in with Dive's denizens.

It didn't take long for her to realize no one in this section would be useful. She muttered a small curse and looked at the back of the room. A large, menacing bouncer stood there with crossed arms and a solid stance. Beside him was a door that doubtless led to somewhere she needed to go.

Voltaic grumbled a curse under her breath and headed for the bartender since that was always where the first payments had to be made to move deeper into places like this.

CHAPTER TWENTY-SIX

Voltaic smiled as she walked up to the bartender. He had wavy gray hair that hung down to his shoulders, a mustache and beard arranged in appropriate piratical style, and wore a white, slightly puffy shirt. She forced herself not to comment on the look, figuring that most people made a buccaneer joke and he wouldn't appreciate it.

She requested, "I'll take a Boost, please." It was a drink that involved a variety of alcohols that she considered pleasant-tasting. The simulation would mimic the effects of alcohol if she chose to let it, but she would never do so on an actual infomancy run.

He slid it in front of her, and she touched it with the end of one red-painted pinky fingernail. Her system scanned it and found a virus inside. She put it back on the bar and pushed it toward the bartender along with a credit chip. "Nice try."

He shrugged. "It's the job. If you can't figure that trap out, you don't belong here."

"I don't think I belong *here*, either." She made a circular gesture in the air with her finger. "How do I get away from the riffraff?"

The bartender tilted his head toward the back of the room. "That's the man you want to talk to. You sure you're up for it?"

She laughed. "Yeah, I think I'll be all right. Thanks." She walked up to the bouncer. "Bartender sent me."

He nodded. "Access to the back is restricted."

"Money? Data? What's the price?"

"Prove yourself worthy." That usually meant a test, either intellectual or physical, or what passed for physical in this place.

Voltaic nodded. "Bring it on."

He opened the door, and she stepped through into a closet-sized room. When the door closed behind her, a door in front of her opened. She stepped forward into an arena. A twelve-foot wall surrounded the combat space with a cage of iron bars overhead.

An audience was present beyond the fighting area, although she imagined it was all computer-generated. Surely no one would want to watch a security test when the Internet offered so much other entertainment.

Implements that could cause damage covered the walls, from simple shovels and pickaxes to exotic martial arts weapons. Voltaic stretched out her fingers and rolled her neck.

Nothing in the simulation was physical. If she got hit, it wouldn't hurt, as such. It wouldn't harm her physical body. Instead, it would slow her connection time in a way analogous to having taken that blow in the real world. There was ultimately no risk in the fight except getting kicked out of the system.

The greatest risk was getting traced back to the real world and having your opponent or enemy come after you there. That had never happened to her, and she operated through too many cutouts for it to happen now. Nothing she'd seen so far suggested this place had the mojo to make it through her firewalls.

An announcer with a deep voice called, "Round one." A door opened across the way and a hulking man stepped out of it. He was easily a foot taller than her and even brawnier than the bouncer had been. His heavy boots looked reinforced, and the armor plates strapped to his shins and thighs were dented but serviceable. He was unclothed from the waist up except for the crimson-stained spiked gauntlets on his fists.

Voltaic rolled her eyes. There was no way this was an enemy infomancer because no one with any self-respect would show up wearing a skin like that. This meant it was a bot.

The program had the advantage of being resident in the system she was visiting, which would make it faster than standard, but at the end of the day it was still a program. Her combined skills and magic should be more than enough to handle it. If they weren't, she'd never be able to show her face here again from the embarrassment of losing.

Voltaic ran toward him as he ran at her. She figured he'd go straight for the knockout blow the way people who buffed themselves up in such a skin normally did. They wanted to show how tough and mighty they were by ending it with one punch. When she got close and he started his move, she slid onto the floor to the side of his legs. The punch he threw at her missed, and he over-balanced.

She came up, stopped her momentum, and jumped at his back. Her twisting elbow strike smashed into the back of his head before he got completely turned around and caused him to stagger forward several steps.

He turned and grabbed her, and his meaty hand snagged her arm. He yanked her and briefly had her close, but she whipped her other hand down to break his grip and dove out of the way. A shoulder roll brought her back to her feet a short distance from him as he shook his head to clear it from the elbow strike.

Next to her on the wall was a Bowie knife. She grabbed it and held it reversed along her right forearm with the pommel down, her fingers wrapped around it, and the dull edge resting against the side of her forearm. When he ran at her again, she sidestepped, brought her free arm up in a circular block, and slashed the knife down and across his side. He bellowed, and she rammed it back before he could move away, sinking the point into the muscle of his stomach.

She yanked it free and spun out of the way before he could grab her. He was bleeding, but whatever passed for adrenaline in this simulation kept him up. If not for the armor, she would've gone for his Achilles tendon or the back of his calves, but those quick-win options weren't available.

Instead, she waited for him to charge again. She took two steps forward when he did and leapt into the air. Her programming made her stronger, faster, and more agile than she could hope to be in normal life, and she cleared his swing by several feet as she somersaulted over him.

Voltaic landed, spun, and slashed the knife across his chest as he turned to face her. Instead of moving away, she stepped inside his guard, rammed the Bowie knife deep into the right side of his chest, then slammed her palm into it to drive it in to the hilt. He staggered back gripping the knife, then pixelated into nothingness. The weapon went with him.

She looked around as if to ask, "Are we done here?" The sound of the door her foe had come through opening again provided her answer. Two more opponents entered. They wore armor over most of their vulnerable spots, although it was patchwork as if from a post-apocalyptic, quasi-medieval movie—knights of the end times.

One carried a rod, the anchor for a chain that ended in a spiked ball. He waved it around two-handed in a figure eight, and she had to admit it moved much faster than she would've preferred.

Spiked balls seemed to be the theme of the day since the other carried two large sticks with menacing spheres at the ends. Despite the size of the weapons, his movements were fast and agile.

Voltaic would've liked to pull her blaster and shoot them both like Indiana Jones in that long-ago film. However, the rules of these tests were as simple as they were unalterable. Only the simulation could increase the violence level.

The only reason she'd been able to use the knife during the last bout was because the enemy had a hand weapon, his armored fists. She couldn't use a ranged weapon until her opponents did. Breaking that rule could get her punished with additional enemies, which wouldn't be a problem, but it could also get her ejected from the place, an outcome she couldn't afford.

She reached up and drew her knives. They were smaller than her forearms but wickedly sharp on both edges and the point. They had a slight crossbar that could catch opponents' weapons, although they wouldn't do a thing against the spiked balls. She'd rely on speed and agility to deal with those.

To that end, she triggered a program. Her avatar's suit held a cornucopia of virtual drugs it could inject into her bloodstream, and she used one to boost her speed and reflexes. In the real world, she was boosting her connection speed. It would only last for a short time before her enemy found a way to shut it down, so she couldn't afford to be passive.

Voltaic charged at the pair. They moved apart so she couldn't hit them both at once, and she angled toward the one on her right, the one with paired weapons. He brought them around in a powerful strike designed to intersect with her head and smash it between them. She went into a low slide between his legs, which were spread for stability during his strike. Her boot shot up into his crotch as she went by, but his armor made the effort useless.

She stomped a foot down and used her remaining momentum to push to her feet, then jumped, spun, and whipped the knife in her right hand around at neck level. Her foe turned quickly enough to see it coming and angled his head. The blade struck his helmet and glanced off.

Voltaic fell instead of landing on her feet and wrenched her body around. Her shins hit the back of his legs, and he went down hard.

His throat was right there, a foot away from her knife. She couldn't follow up on the attack because the ball on the end of the chain slammed down where her head would've been if she hadn't moved. She surged up and ran to get distance from them, inwardly cursing their speed. They might be bots, but they were good ones.

The one she'd knocked to the ground stood, shook his head as if she'd rung his bell a little, and stalked her from one side as her other opponent did so in the opposite direction. Two-on-one wasn't pretty.

She shoved one knife into its sheath and grabbed a sword from the wall. It would give her the advantage of range and was of a weight she could manipulate one-handed. Not perfectly, even with the buzz of her enhanced abilities still present, but well enough.

This time, she bolted toward the one with the ball on the chain. She charged around to his far side to put him in between her and the other attacker. He whipped the weapon around toward her head, as she'd expected. Both seemed to want the fast, fancy kill shot.

Voltaic shoved the sword up in its way and the chain wrapped around the blade. She stabbed her knife up, locking it through one of the thick links and trapping his weapon. Then she yanked hard.

He stumbled forward when he refused to let go. She skipped in, made a rigid plane with her right hand, the first digit of each finger curled under, and drove her knuckles into his throat. He choked, gagged, then disappeared. His weapon did too, and she caught her knife as it fell.

She turned to the other with a smile. He seemed dubious, but she twitched her knife at him. "Come on." He did.

She blocked his first strike outward with her sword, blocked the second outward with the forearm of her knife hand against the stick, then delivered a jumping kick to the bottom of his chin. His head rocked back, and as soon as she landed, she stabbed both of her blades into his neck. He vanished, as did her sword.

"Damn," she muttered as she looked around for another weapon, hoping the fight was over but doubting that it was. The fanfare as three enemies stepped into the arena confirmed her suspicions.

CHAPTER TWENTY-SEVEN

The trio spread apart as they advanced so she couldn't get to them with a single attack. The bots were dressed as ninjas out of a movie with black outfits and masks and wicked-looking weapons. The one on her left had two straight swords and the one on the right had a long chain with a gleaming blade on the end. The one in the center caught her eye. He had tiny knives in his hands, too small for hand-to-hand combat.

Voltaic grinned, feinted to the right, then dashed to the left. The blade on the chain that whistled through the air at her would've caught her if she'd kept moving to the right. It met only air and whistled again as her foe pulled it back as quickly as he'd hurled it.

She wasn't lucky enough to evade all the attacks. One of the throwing knives dug deep into her shoulder and rendered her right arm useless. It would have been a problem in the last fight, but the rules had changed for the better.

Voltaic laughed as she reached across with her left hand

and awkwardly pulled the blaster out of her holster. She shook her head at the one in the middle. "Stupid move escalating, buddy." She pulled the trigger, and a bolt of energy leapt out of the pistol, slammed into him, and reduced him to pixels.

The other two charged her with furious cries of rage, but she blasted each in turn, rendering them and their wicked weapons into nothingness.

When no additional enemies appeared, she pulled the knife out of her shoulder and tossed it aside. The wound disappeared immediately, as did the weapon. She transferred the gun to her right hand, shoved it back into its holster, and yelled, "All right. I've played your game. Let me out of here."

A door that hadn't been there a moment before opened in the side wall. She sauntered through it with her thumbs hooked into her belt and entered a hallway. A dozen steps took her to another door into a room much like the one she'd visited topside but executed with opulence rather than kitschiness.

Golden softwoods abounded, and the displays showed neutral scenes of the ocean rather than displaying the sea creatures she'd seen above. They also served as primary illumination. The whole place seemed like it was underwater with rippling lights from the waves on the monitors. It held fewer tables, and more were occupied by a single individual than in the previous room.

The bar was also nicer, a complete circle of glass and chrome rather than the straight-line standard wood of the one above. The woman standing behind it was dressed as a buccaneer in a bright red tunic with golden buttons. A black leather bandolier held a holster with a flintlock pistol. Her brunette hair defied gravity in its elaborate, presumably period-appropriate styling.

Voltaic claimed a stool. "Does that outfit have a sword?"

The woman grinned as she set her hands on the bar and leaned forward. Her teeth were perfect. "You'd pay to find out."

Voltaic laughed. "I'm not your type?"

The bartender grinned wider. "You'd pay to find out that, too."

Voltaic raised her hands. "Okay, you win." She lowered them and said more quietly, "I'm looking for some work."

The other woman nodded and matched the level and tone of Voltaic's words. "You've come to the right place."

"Any suggestions?" Voltaic slid a gold coin across the bar, appropriate for the theme of this particular simulation.

The bartender swept it up with a deft move that made it look like a magic trick. "What are you into?"

Voltaic raised an eyebrow. "You'll pay to find out." They laughed together, then she continued, "Whatever pays the best."

The bartender nodded. "That's the answer of a professional. Everyone in here pays more than average and expects the same of those they hire, but if you're looking for big bucks and big challenges, there are two. The man in the back left corner wearing the fedora has a reputation as a go-between for wet work. The woman at the far end of the bar has a rep for complex operations that require more finesse than fedora guy."

The bartender probably knew their handles, but such information had to be earned, not shared.

Voltaic nodded. "Good to know. Thanks." She slipped two more coins across the bar and stood. Her gaze focused on the man, but her systems gave her nothing solid on him, only some rumors attached to the fedora.

She doubted he was the one who'd set up the action against Damien Zane. Someone acting as an intermediary for killings probably wasn't likely to put together the sophisticated operation that seemed to be underway. Too direct a thinker. She might be wrong and would probably get something out of meeting him anyway, so she wouldn't waste the opportunity.

She stood beside his table. "May I?" He nodded permission, and she sat across from him. He was thick but strong, dressed in a dark suit, shirt, and tie with big rings on both hands and the fedora with the rakish tilt over his dark hair.

His voice was gravelly as he asked, "What are you looking for?"

"Work. Something that pays well."

"Are you squeamish?"

"Not interested in anything that involves harming puppies or kids, if that's what you're asking."

He chuckled. "Nothing so innocent. I have scruples. Not many, but some. I'm Charlie."

She nodded. "Nice to meet you, Charlie. I'm V."

"Like the letter?"

"Just like."

He squinted a little. "What's it stand for?"

Voltaic gave him the smile of someone who'd baited a

trap and watched it snap closed. "Now if I wanted you to know that I probably would've told you, wouldn't I have?"

He leveled a finger at her as he laughed. "Good point. I'm going to call you Vixen."

She rolled her eyes. "As in a sexy lady or as in a reindeer? I'm not sure the latter is a compliment."

Charlie laughed. "You'll never know. What are your talents?"

"My team is good at snatch and grabs, break-ins, that kind of thing."

"I have some of that at times, but not right now. Check in now and again and let me know if you're interested in anything more serious. I like the look of you, kid."

"Thanks, Chuck."

He laughed as he leaned back in his chair to watch her stand. "Until next time, Vixen."

Voltaic headed across the room and sat on a stool away from the woman the bartender had mentioned. She was willowy with pale blonde hair and skin of a similar shade, and clad in a little black dress. Her face seemed too serious for the rest of her look. The woman asked, "Have a nice conversation with our fedora-wearing friend?"

Voltaic waggled her fingers. "Not exactly."

"Oh? Mismatch?"

"He has jobs that require brawn instead of brains. It's not that I'm lacking either, just that I prefer a challenge."

The other woman laughed. "Definitely a mismatch, then. I'm Lash."

She held out a hand. "V."

Lash shook it. "Good to meet you, V. What kind of challenges are you looking for?" Voltaic repeated what she'd told Charlie. Lash asked, "Any problems with snatch and grabs where humans are the target?"

She shrugged to show her lack of concern. "Not if the pay's right, as long as they're not children or anything."

"No, I won't represent people who want that. Just adults, and usually scumbags, at that."

"Ransoms?"

Lash sighed as if that was an issue of frustration for her. "They always say that's the plan when they talk with me. It's difficult to tell who means it until everything is over, you know? Sometimes things go bad unexpectedly. Sometimes that was the plan all along."

Voltaic nodded. "Kidnapping for profit isn't really all that easy to get away with these days."

"True that."

She leaned closer. "I've heard through the grapevine that someone out there is paying a bonus for success. Which says to me they have multiple teams working and that they have a lot of money. Seems like that would be someone who's going after ransom. I know my team is better than anyone they might have in mind."

The other woman nodded. "Yeah, I have a piece of that. Did some organizing. I agree. The principal was certainly able to put down the deposit fast enough."

Voltaic did her best not to show her excitement at the connection. "Any chance I could get into that?"

She doubted it, and Lash's next words confirmed it. "No, sorry. Current roster is all full on that one."

Voltaic laughed as if it didn't matter. "Damn. How many beat me?"

Lash considered her. "You know I can't say." As she spoke, she spread the fingers on her right hand.

Voltaic got the message. Five. She flipped her hand around like a magician and a business card appeared in it. She handed it to the other woman. "If anything opens up, definitely give me a yell."

Lash nodded. "Will do. Check in from time to time."

Voltaic nodded, then cut her connection. The real world filled her vision again as she leaned back in her chair. "Well, that was mostly useless. Damn." She recorded a verbal report of the encounter, since all real-time recordings were blocked in Dive, and sent it to Zack. "Time for bed, I guess."

She considered for a second, then went to the fridge and got another energy drink. She returned to her chair. "All right. Maybe I can get some information on those two in the bar, and that'll lead somewhere. Can't hurt to look."

CHAPTER TWENTY-EIGHT

Just like that, it was the day of the concert. The previous days had passed in a haze of watching rehearsals, gathering their gear, working on the warehouse facility, and searching everywhere for information about who might be targeting Damien. They'd come up with nothing.

Derek and Voltaic had put their heads together. The only thing that came out of it was that there were five groups at first, meaning there were now three if they could believe Voltaic's contact. The infomancer put that likelihood at sixty-forty for. On the one hand, the woman had a reputation to uphold. On the other, she could have been screwing with them for fun.

Danica's team gathered at the warehouse at noon. The lenses hadn't arrived yet, so they'd be wearing glasses. Maybe the fact that the other security wouldn't be wearing them would help to keep them somewhat anonymous. She, Alexandra, and Zack sat near their lockers, arranged in a U shape with benches in front of them.

Jilly flew from the top of one locker to the top of the next repeatedly, as if she was eager to get moving. The lockers were triple normal size, easily large enough to handle all the gear they might have. Right now they seemed empty.

She and the others wore the black cargo pants and black T-shirts of the security detail for the concert. A heavier outer shirt would go on over the body armor, also emblazoned with their status as security. Alexandra commented, "We might need something better than this in the future, uniform-wise."

Danica replied, "Agreed. We'll figure it out for the next one. This one came a little fast for things to be perfect."

Zack asked, "Not too fast, though?"

"More people on the ground for this would've been better, but the band has security, too. I think we're adequate to the challenge."

Jilly piped up, "More than adequate. Impressive. Stupendous." Everyone laughed.

Zack replied, "I like your attitude."

Jilly did the wing wave she used when she was happy.

Danica reached into her locker and pulled out the body armor. It fastened down the left-hand side after going over her head and fit like a second skin. It was heavier than she'd anticipated, although Alexandra said it was lighter than most of the bulletproof vests she'd worn. Danica had only used those on a couple of occasions for short intervals, so she had no other experience to draw upon.

Her Glock 19 pistol, loaded with frangible rounds, went into a holster at the small of her back. It would be underneath the button-up shirt they would all leave untucked. She tucked the extra magazine with frangible anti-magic rounds into a pocket.

An equipment belt was fastened tight around her waist, which the shirt would also hide. It held a Taser, several grenades, a small emergency medical kit, and her healing and energy potions. A communication pack that interfaced with the glasses rode on one side.

Voltaic had reiterated that with all the signals going on inside the venue, including the wireless guitars, micro-phones, monitors, and such, it would be good to have extra power for their communications system. Danica wasn't going to argue with the infomancer about anything involving technology.

Another thing Voltaic had insisted on was that each of them carry a tracker. Danica slipped the small disc into the tiny pocket on the tongue of her boot. The device would allow Voltaic to keep track of their positions inside the venue, which could prove useful if one of them got knocked out or something.

While she waited for the others to finish dressing, she activated a direct channel to Voltaic. "What do you think?"

"I've had a drone overhead all day scanning in thermal, normal, and motion detection modes. Everything seems fine. They have a little encampment backstage with the tour buses and trucks all blocked in like it was at the prac-tice site. They also have several SUVs inside that little compound."

Danica scowled. "I don't remember that being part of the plan."

"Nor do I. I contacted their security and asked why the

vehicles were there. They said they'd discuss it with you when you arrived."

Danica pinched the bridge of her nose. "I'm not sure I'm cut out to work with celebrities."

Voltaic laughed. "Boy, have you chosen the wrong job, then."

She laughed and returned her attention to the others in the room. "Are you guys ready yet?"

Jilly flew over and landed on her shoulder. "Always."

Zack replied, "Yep."

Alexandra nodded. "I'm thinking of all the other things we could bring to this that might prove useful."

Danica asked, "Like what?"

"A tank. A really big tank. With a machine gun on top."

She laughed. "You can take the woman out of the Army, but you can't take the Army out of the woman."

"True that."

Danica opened a portal, and they stepped through into the back of the venue. She'd visited the day before to look over things as they began their load-in. Normally, the setup would be on the same day as the show. Because this was the first warmup night of the tour, they'd wanted time to address challenges and do a dry run for the technical side.

She walked over to the head of security, Michael Prescott, who stood with the stage manager. They both looked nervous at their approach, which didn't bode well. "Gentlemen."

Seth Jasik handed over lanyards with badges. "Here are your passes. Keep them visible at all times. They're electronically coded to get you through checkpoints and such."

Danica nodded, put hers around her neck, and handed the others off.

Jilly asked, "What, none for me?"

"Could you wear one, or would it throw off your flying?"

"Don't know. Never tried."

She patted the dragon on the head with two fingers. "We'll look into it for next time."

That satisfied the dragon, so Danica turned her attention to the head of security and asked as calmly as she could manage, "Why are there SUVs here?"

His face crinkled in a pained wince. "He's insisting on the jet."

She shook her head. "No."

He shrugged. "I don't know what to tell you. We used all the logic in the world with them, and he doesn't care. It's superstition, I guess. But he's taking the jet."

Danica gritted her teeth. Arthur had warned her that it would be like this sometimes, but she'd thought survival instincts would keep the rock star from doing anything this stupid. She forced out, "Fine. For now." Then she turned away before she indulged her desire to throw a fireball at the SUVs and ensure they couldn't be used.

Prescott's words stopped her. "One other thing."

Danica turned slowly and fought to keep her face and tone neutral. "Yes?"

"There will be a red carpet."

"You're freaking kidding me."

Prescott shook his head. "No. The media requested it, and Damien's PR team agreed."

Alexandra asked, "Who's in charge, them or you?"

"We exist in an atmosphere of mutual dislike. Unfortunately, when we disagree, Damien's voice sounds loudest."

Danica decided not to fight it. As Arthur had warned, sometimes the client would do things that were bad for them, and all they could do was try their best to ensure their safety. "Fine. We escort him."

Prescott replied, "Fine. The rest of the band?"

"I don't think they're in imminent danger, so you can take care of them."

"Good. I'll keep you in the loop on the timing."

She looked at Alexandra and Zack. Each carried a case. "All right. We'll set up inside. Then we'll deal with the red carpet.

"Divide the sensors and cameras between you. Zack, you go high. Alexandra, you handle the venue's main floor. Anywhere you think we need eyes and sensors, put them in place. If anyone bothers you, wave your pass at them. If they keep bothering you, call me. I'll have Jilly fire blast them."

The little dragon interjected, "Fun!"

They walked together into the venue, and the other two set about splitting up the equipment. Danica added, "Zack, you're in charge of picking these up afterward. We can't afford to buy new ones every time. Alexandra and I will escort Rockstar after the concert."

Alexandra scowled. "To the jet."

"That's an open question. I might just throw him through a portal and be done with it."

Alexandra laughed. "How much do you hate being in here?" She gestured at the arena, but Danica knew what she was referring to.

"I'm functional without my magic, but I'll admit it feels like part of me is missing. It's uncomfortable."

Alexandra nodded. "I can see that. It won't hinder you, though?"

"Only in that my desire is to put a shield around him, then another, and another still, and keep them there for the whole show. But no, I'll be fine."

She walked along the venue's floor as the others turned to their tasks. Workers were setting up rows of folding chairs inside the large, chalked-out sections. The front third of the space had no chairs, presumably for general admission. According to Voltaic, the fans were already lined up outside and had been doing so since five in the morning.

The good news was that the band's security would walk with the band members as they moved down the runway surrounded by the general admission audience. Any normal fan wouldn't be able to hurt anyone in the band. The venue's scanning should hopefully address anyone who tried to bring in a weapon. The anti-magic emitter took more dangerous and less visible threats off the table. It should be fine.

Danica laughed inwardly at the realization that she was trying to convince herself things were okay. A walk through the concourse showed way too many workers around already, who hopefully had been scanned as the guests would be, and far too many places where someone looking for trouble could hide. She muttered, "I hate this."

Alexandra replied, "Yeah, not a fan either."

Zack countered, "From above, it's kind of peaceful."

Danica walked back into the arena and looked up. He

was walking along the girders that made up the grid stretching across the entire venue. He waved. She warned, "Don't fall."

He chuckled. "I borrowed a harness from the rigging team. I have a safety line, and they're also going to give me a perfectly measured rope line so if I need to get down from here in a hurry, I can."

"Good thinking."

"I'm not just a pretty face, boss, even though that's why you hired me."

She snorted, and Alexandra laughed.

Voltaic interjected, "Ah, the old Zack charm. Now I know everything will be all right."

Danica replied, "From your words to the universe's ears."

Voltaic's tone changed. "Red carpet imminent. The SUV with the band is three blocks away."

Danica gritted her teeth again at the fact that they weren't using magical transport, even though it didn't make sense with a red carpet arrival. "Give me a path." A line illuminated in her display glasses, and she followed it out a side door.

She walked the red carpet in the wrong direction, ignoring the shouted questions and comments as she wrapped herself in shields. Jilly launched from her shoulder and flew around to watch for trouble. When she reached the end, she smiled at Prescott and growled, "Let me guess, he'll need to touch them."

"Of course he will. It's what he does."

She held in an exasperated sigh. "Okay. Here's the deal. If I see any kind of a threat, he and I are vanishing. I'll hide us, then portal him inside where it's safe. If he argues, I'll use my Taser on him. Do you have any problem with that?"

His face said he did, but he replied, "No. Do what you have to do."

More calmly, she added, "Remember, if he gets ticked, blame it on me."

Prescott laughed. "I've been doing a lot of that."

The SUVs turned a corner into view of the crowd. They started screaming in earnest, and her earplugs automatically dimmed the noise. Hidden signs came out, but no one appeared to have weapons or ill intent. Danica pushed magic into her senses and muscles and willed the car to drive faster.

It didn't. It was almost as if it was deliberately trying to infuriate her. She was sure someone had cast a spell to slow time. Finally, it arrived like a glacier spreading southward. She stood next to the back door and watched the crowd.

The door opened, and Damien jumped out and raised his fists. The crowd went wild. She fought off the urge to backhand him in the stomach and walked in front of him as he moved down the carpet. The drone view in her glasses showed her his positioning. A moment later, Voltaic added several live streams from people's phones that gave better views.

One person jumped the cordon in front of her and tried to rush Damien. Danica interposed herself, then did so again as the woman tried to evade her. Damien stepped forward and hugged the woman anyway.

Finally, she got him inside. Prescott had been walking

behind him. She faced him. "He's yours for now." Then she stomped off to cool down.

Voltaic said, "Nice job."

"Yeah, but I need to chill out a bit, or this nice job will kill me."

The infomancer laughed. "All this and we haven't even soundchecked yet."

Danica tapped the healing potion at her waist, thinking she might need it to deal with the headache she was developing. One named Damien Zane.

CHAPTER TWENTY-NINE

Jilly landed on her shoulder as she entered the venue. Danica tried to drop her off in a comfortable and out-of-the-way spot, worried that the noise would be too loud when the music started. Jilly said she'd be fine and not to worry. Danica couldn't do anything but take her at her word.

Danica walked the interior with Jilly riding on her shoulder as she inspected the camera and sensor installations. It all looked good. A bustle at the stage culminated in the band arriving for their sound check. Danica listened as she continued to walk. She had to admit they sounded good.

Voltaic advised, "You have an hour and a half before doors open. That's good relaxation time. Once the fans come in, Prescott suggests you should be backstage."

Danica asked, "Anyone have a counterargument?" No one did, so they found the crew's lounge area and took advantage of the empty couches while they worked.

The energy backstage grew increasingly palpable as the

start of the main show neared. The opening act had performed and done its job of firing up the crowd. Damien and his band gathered together as assistants secured boxes on their clothes and helped them get their earplugs situated. Techs stood nearby with musical instruments for the guitarists. Stage managers ran around doing things.

Danica moved up to Damien and tucked the tracker she'd removed from her boot into the front pocket of his leather pants while he was distracted. It was foolish for them not to have put one on him in the first place. *Lesson learned. Won't make that mistake again.*

Seth Jasik walked up to Damien. "You ready?"

"Too ready, brother. Let's make some noise."

A moment later, the lights went out in the venue, and the crowd screamed. The intro song began to play as the light show started, and the screams increased. The band members were virtually bouncing. All wore wide grins.

Damien caught her looking and gestured broadly at everything. "This is what it's all about. Us. The fans. That give-and-take, the energy. So much energy." He shook his head as if he didn't have the superlatives he needed. "You'll see."

Security got in line. Two went ahead of the band. Alexandra came next, then the band, then two more security guards. Danica took the rear. Zack was already in the girders.

Voltaic was watching, as evidenced by the way the window in Danica's display dedicated to the feeds from the cameras they'd placed kept changing. The infomancer had offered more, but Danica thought too many would be distracting.

The stage manager arrived at the head of the line and started to move. Everyone followed like ducklings. Alexandra turned away before they reached the side of the stage, and the band split off to go on to the stage from the side while Danica walked out to the front corner. Alexandra emerged from the opposite side and took her position at the other front corner.

Zack muttered, "This is awesome," as the intro song wrapped up.

Silence hung for several seconds, then the pyrotechnics went off to start the show, and the first chords rang out into the auditorium. Firecrackers, sparklers, and flames shot up behind the band as they dashed onto the stage. Danica had known it was coming, but it was still a shock to the senses.

Danica forced herself to focus on the crowd. It required substantial effort to keep her eyes away from the stage during the first song, but keeping her attention on the audience as the concert continued became easier. It helped that she didn't know Damien's songs and wasn't lulled into singing along like the rest of the audience and some of his security.

The first tense moment came when Damien danced down the runway. Fans pressed against the barricades surrounding it, reaching toward him only a body length away. The barricades were too low to stop anyone who wanted to get over them, but they provided a clear space for security to move with Damien and do their jobs.

Damien reached out and slapped hands with people as he sang, then made like he was going to jump down.

Screaming ensued, but he twirled and danced to the stage instead.

Alexandra commented, "He knows how to work the crowd, that's for sure."

Danica replied, "He's gonna give me a heart attack."

She looked over her shoulder and spotted the slight haze that covered Jilly at the back of the stage. Her natural camouflage worked even with the anti-magic field present, as did whatever magic protected her hearing. Danica wondered how that worked and if being fundamentally magical made the difference.

Halfway through, during one of Damien's most popular songs, fans rushed the stage from the sides.

Alexandra blocked a couple by putting herself in their path, but a few more made it up to the stage and ran toward Damien. Security looked like they'd done this a hundred times before as they picked each one off before they could reach him and carried them off the stage.

Voltaic advised, "That's normal stuff, Prescott says. Nothing to worry about. They generally just want hugs."

Danica growled, "I hope those metal detectors found all the knives that might've come into the venue. If you're close enough to hug, you're close enough to stab."

Alexandra added, "There's always steak knives from the restaurant."

"You're not helping."

Zack interjected, "I'm all rigged up here. If you need me to jump down and land on somebody's head, I can do it. Might even be able to manage a Tarzan swing across the stage to rescue Damien."

Danica resisted putting her head in her hands. "I can

only imagine the insurance claim when you break him with your man of the apes impersonation."

"Are you suggesting I'm not the most agile of humans?"

"That's exactly how I would've put it, actually."

He laughed. "Such a lack of faith. Sad."

The tensest moment came when Damien jumped off the runway. He ran along the barricade with his microphone in one hand, doing fist bumps, high-fives, and occasional hugs with the fans. It didn't escape her notice that the scantily clad female fans generally got the longest hugs. She shrugged and figured that was part of what made Rockstar, Rockstar.

She followed his security as he worked her side. Once they reached the front of the runway and curved around the other side, Alexandra took point and led them while Danica returned to her position. She'd hoped Damien would listen to her advice and not be so close to the crowd but had known from the start that it was unlikely at best.

Finally, the band played the last song of the main set. They said thank you and good night, then proceeded off the stage. The crowd immediately started to chant, and the fact that the house lights didn't come up cued them into the fact that an encore was planned.

Danica followed the band into a backstage area that was even more frenetic than at the show's start. People took instruments from the band members, each of whom went into their dressing room and closed the door behind them. The crowd's chanting rattled some of the equipment.

Danica watched over her side of the backstage area while Alexandra stayed on the opposite side. Jilly and Zack were still inside the main part of the venue, watching over the crowd. Danica was relieved that there'd been no attack. Still, a cynical voice in her head wondered how long they'd have to stay with the band until something broke and they figured out who was behind this so they could be done with this gig.

Like any little kid, she had dreamed of being a rock star, but her end of this operation wasn't nearly as glamorous as her fantasies of it had been. The band members emerged one after the next and headed for a table with drinks and cups labeled with their names.

Danica nodded toward them and asked Prescott, who was standing nearby, "They're safe?"

He nodded. "I watched over them myself. New bottles. New mixers. No worries."

"Oh, I have lots of worries. Trust me."

The band members came over to the table, and each lifted the cup with their name. They clinked the plastic cups, said cheers, and drank them down. Damien shouted, "Ready to give the people what they want?"

Each of the others responded in the affirmative with a raised fist. That was the moment the attackers burst into action. Security moved at the same time Voltaic yelled a warning in her earpieces. Danica snapped her head to the left and saw three men with pistols in their hands, all pointed at the band. They pulled the triggers and soft pops emanated from the weapons' suppressors.

Band security jumped on the musicians and brought them crashing down on the table, which collapsed underneath them. Grunts of pain told her that some of the bullets had connected. Danica hoped the band's security had taken her suggestion that they should wear bulletproof vests underneath their clothes to heart.

As her brain processed everything, her body drew her gun and prepared to fire. Her hip swiveled as she brought the pistol up. Her eyes caught the sight as her other hand joined the first, and it rose to center mass on one of her foes. She pulled the trigger and that one dropped.

The others swung their weapons toward the new threat, and she dove behind a rack of audio equipment from the opening act. Bullets smacked into the case but fortunately didn't penetrate.

Danica grabbed a flash-bang grenade from her belt, primed it, and hurled it down the hallway toward the attackers. Her earplugs dimmed the sound, and she closed her eyes until the bright flash detectable through them was gone. Then she ran toward them, drawing her Taser with her off hand, and triggered it at the one on the left with some thought of taking them for interrogation later.

The man staggered and went down. The other one got a shot off at her that struck her in the chest.

The body armor was as good as Simon had promised it would be. The impact knocked her slightly off stride, so the shoulder slam she meant to put into his face hit him in the chest instead. He staggered backward, and she lifted her leg and stomped down hard on his shin. The bone broke, and he fell with a scream.

She kicked his gun away from him, then grabbed those of the other two and threw them aside as well. Only then did she look up and discover that another fight was going on.

Alexandra had moved into cover the moment she saw the five attackers dressed as venue workers appear on her side of the room. She shot one as they advanced but had to scurry around her cover as they dashed past her position. She shot another one as she came out from behind the group but only winged him as he moved at the last instant. He stopped and raised his pistol, forcing her into action and allowing the other three to keep advancing.

She skipped into range, blocked his arm upward before he could pull the trigger, and punched him in the face with the pistol in her hand. His round went into the rafters as blood spurted from his face and his free hand instinctively went up to hold it. She put the barrel of her pistol against his thigh and pulled the trigger.

He went down with a scream and a giant hole in his leg. She kicked his gun away and shoved hers into its holster as she dashed for the remaining three. They were already engaged in hand-to-hand with the band's security, who, to their credit, had charged in fast enough to deny the attackers a shot along the way.

She amended that thought when she spotted a security person on the floor with blood leaking from his shoulder. At least they only got one.

Alexandra angled at the nearest enemy, already engaged with a member of the band's security, and yanked him backward by his shoulder. He reacted faster than she anticipated, whipping around with the momentum of her pull to throw a roundhouse punch at her face that she leaned back to avoid. It grazed her cheek but did no damage.

He'd left himself open for a counter. She landed a fist in his ribs, then jumped to clear his raised shoulder and punch down at his face. Her fist connected with his temple and he dropped hard to the floor.

Another attacked as she landed. She spun away, but not fast enough to avoid a kick in the hip that knocked her to the floor. She bounced back up, adrenaline firing her muscles, and circled to find an angle on him. That gave her a view of the first one she'd shot as he got to his feet and ran to join the melee. She snapped a curse about his body armor, then shouted, "Danica," forgetting that she didn't have to yell to be heard over the comms.

Alexandra hoped her partner would come to join the fight but couldn't wait to see. One of the attackers had brought a knife and was skilled enough with it that his first strike almost landed in the spot between her armor and her armpit. It would have with a normal bulletproof vest, but the custom body armor covered more. The impact still stung.

She blocked, punched, and dodged as he slashed at her, and it was all she could do to hold her own. When they changed positions, she saw Danica engaged with another halfway across the backstage area and not about to pull off an imminent rescue. At that moment, one of the bad guys pulled Rockstar to his feet and forced him to run toward the exit with a gun to the back of his head.

Alexandra yelled, "Danica!"

At the same time, Danica yelled, "Jilly!"

Jilly had leapt into flight at the sound of the first gunshots. She didn't have a direct line to backstage from her position and was forced to fly a circular path. She automatically chose Danica's side of the venue and discovered she was some distance from Danica, who had moved toward the center.

Danica pointed and shouted, "Get him."

Jilly saw that a man with a weapon at the back of Damien's head was forcing Rockstar to run. The dragon flapped as fast as she could in pursuit. At top speed, she was twice as fast as the men were running, so she closed the distance quickly.

She had flown through the entire arena beforehand to understand the territory and knew this corridor extended to the outside. It also had an intersection ahead that the attacker might take to go farther into the venue or out a different door into the back.

Her first instinct was to blast them both with lightning. It wouldn't be damaging in the long term, and she could keep blasting the bad guy once she'd separated him from the good guy. She refrained, worried that the blast might cause the attacker's muscles to contract and pull the trigger on the weapon. Instead, she flew in from behind, bit him on the side of the neck, and clawed him near his throat.

He shouted in rage and surprise and slashed his free hand at her, but Jilly dodged it easily and bit his cheek. He didn't stop to fight and didn't resist other than with the blindly waving arm, so she kept attacking him. He bent his head when she went for his eye.

It wasn't a stalemate, and she'd get something vital eventually, but a look ahead told her she didn't have enough time for that strategy. She had to do something else to stop him but had no idea what that might be.

Zack solved that problem as he barreled into the intersection and tackled Rockstar. He spun and shielded the other man with his body as he slammed into the far wall, then took him to the floor. That was all the space Jilly needed.

She breathed lightning onto the man who'd attacked Damien. Her breath weapons weren't quite as powerful as those of a full-size dragon, but they were far stronger than one would expect from a dragon her size. He shivered and staggered, then fell.

She did it again and held it there until his eyes rolled back in his head. Then, just because she could and he deserved it, she gave him one more blast and the worst insult she could think of. "Stupid jerk."

Danica had finished taking down the attacker who prevented her from chasing Damien when Rockstar pelted back up the hallway with Zack and Jilly at his side. As soon as Damien was near enough, he shouted, "Is the band okay?"

His security people assured him they were, and the band members stuck their heads out of the dressing rooms they'd been pushed into. Prescott urged, "We have to get you all out of here, right now."

Danica had a moment of pure appreciation for the band's head of security. *Finally, someone talking sense.*

Damien shook his head and called for the others to get

a move on. "No way. We owe the fans an encore. We're going back out." He ran past his stunned security. The band followed, the guitarists snatching their instruments as they went by.

Danica stared at Alexandra, who rolled her eyes. Then they ran for their positions in the arena since Damien had once again done something stupid and perfectly in character for a true rock star.

CHAPTER THIRTY

If the adventure backstage had rattled any band members, they didn't show it. The encore was maximum energy. Damien worked the crowd, who repaid him with vocal adoration. During the last verse of the final song, confetti cannons showered the crowd with heart-shaped paper, and the band exited to earthquake-level applause.

Danica tensed as they reached the backstage area, but no threat materialized. The band went into their dressing rooms to do whatever musicians did after the show. She left Alexandra and Jilly watching over them as she checked the compound in the venue's rear. Prescott had told her the band would want to decompress in the tour bus for a while before Damien headed for the jet.

She saw no threats but asked, "Voltaic, do you see anything back here?"

"Nothing that shouldn't be there. Some crew members. They've been in and out all evening." When the band emerged, she walked with them out toward the bus, surreptitiously putting shields around them all now that she was free of the anti-magic emitter's interference.

Three portals opened without warning, including one right behind them, and people flowed out from them. Danica's inner voice growled, *The fifth group,* and she acted.

Everyone surged into motion. This time, Danica took charge of Rockstar. She layered additional shields around them both and pushed him down behind the front panel of one of the SUVs he thought would take him to a plane. She snorted inwardly. There was no way she was letting him get on a plane.

A bullet slammed into her body armor, and she snarled a curse and ducked farther. "Anti-magic ammunition. Be careful. My shields aren't enough."

An enemy with a rifle moved to get an angle on her. Jilly blasted him with lightning before he could shoot, and he went down. The dragon was visible when she attacked but still had her veil working when she didn't.

Danica instinctively knew where she was at all times and sensed it as the dragon circled to take on another attacker. She used force magic to rip weapons out of people's hands and focused on countering magical attacks and protecting Damien.

Alexandra and Zack took shots from behind improvised cover, and their anti-magic ammo cut the attackers' numbers in rapid succession. It didn't take long to defeat the assault, although another security member went down during the fight. The medics who had been working hard since the fracas backstage rushed out to attend to him.

After everyone on her team confirmed it was safe, Danica stood and pulled Rockstar by the arm to stand in a circle with his head of security, Alexandra, and Zack. Danica stated as calmly as she could manage, "You're not going on your plane."

Rockstar spoke in his best offended English accent. "I am going on my plane. Right now, there are fans waiting for me on the tarmac in Cincinnati. I'm not going to disappoint them by not showing up."

Danica looked at the security chief, who shrugged. She opened a portal, used force magic to lift a loudly protesting and thrashing Damien Zane off his feet, and levitated him through to the warehouse. She snapped, "Zack, Alexandra, stay with them."

Alexandra fished in her belt and tossed a disc tracker to Danica. Danica nodded. "Thanks." She closed the portal before Damien could get up from where she'd dropped him. Prescott shook his head. "That's not going to make him happy."

"I absolutely do not care. We can get him safely to the Cincinnati airport. He can still get his fix of adoration. Alexandra and Zack will call Arthur and get it done."

He nodded. "What are you going to do now?"

She focused her magic and cast a spell. Her image rippled and was replaced by Damien's from his long hair to his rock 'n' roll boots and everything in between. She appeared to be dressed in his shirt and jacket while he'd been topless when she'd thrown him through the portal. She replied in her magically accurate English accent, "I'm gonna take the jet and see my fans."

She climbed into the SUV, wrapped herself and the driver in shields, and kept an eye out for trouble as the motorcade rolled to the airport. As she'd expected, nothing happened. It seemed like they were trying to capture Damien, and randomly attacking a fast-moving vehicle wasn't a productive method.

When the idea of impersonating him had slammed into her head out of nowhere, she'd judged the potential trouble points would be boarding the jet and when it landed. Whatever it was, she and Jilly would deal with it.

The dragon was in the inner pocket of her jacket, resting. Using her breath weapon was tiring. Danica had given her many compliments and lots of praise for saving Rockstar, and the dragon had drunk it in like the sweetest nectar. At least one of them was relaxed.

What she was doing was fairly stupid in the grand scheme of things, and Arthur would probably have opinions about it. She couldn't think of a better way to get at who was behind this than to allow Rockstar to be captured, and it couldn't be Damien at risk. She tucked the tracker into her boot. At least Voltaic had double measures to track her even if everything else went wrong.

Her comms were still working, and she listened as things wound down for everyone else. Rockstar was upset, but they'd get him to Cincinnati soon enough. He could always appear at the airport once the jet landed.

She was prepared to cast a portal in an instant, the magic held ready. It needed only a word and a gesture to bring it into existence. Other than the first shot at him during the morning concert, everything had pointed to capture as the goal. At worst, maybe there was a higher bounty for capturing than killing him. All in all, she felt reasonably safe from random death at the moment.

After a short time at cruising altitude, Voltaic reported, "You're off course."

Danica frowned, went forward to ask the flight crew what was up, and discovered an empty cockpit. The aircraft was being remotely piloted, and the announcements had been AI or transmitted from the ground.

She shared that information with Voltaic, who asked, "Do you want me to try to hack it?"

Danica looked around the plane as she considered her options. "No. As long as I have my magic, I can get free easily. I have Jilly here with me, too. Just keep an eye on me and be ready to send in the cavalry."

"I'll coordinate with Arthur."

"Perfect."

After a fairly short time aloft, the jet landed at a small regional airport in Michigan. The infomancer had kept her updated on things throughout the flight. Danica stowed her display glasses in a pocket and sat calmly as five men in suits boarded the plane, brandished guns, and demanded she obey them. She protested as she thought Damien would, even got up and tried some threats that went nowhere, and then allowed herself to be handcuffed.

She'd expected a magical would show up to transport her. Instead, they put a bag over her head and dragged her into a car. During the ride, she impersonated Rockstar as best she could with lots of protests, occasional offers to pay them more than someone else was paying them, and entreaties to "Think about the fans, man." None of it worked.

When they reached their destination, she was escorted up some steps, through what sounded like interior rooms, then pushed down on her knees. Someone pulled the bag off her head, and she blinked at the brightness of the well-appointed room. She took in the gold records in frames, the cabinets full of other awards, and the expensive furniture.

Then her gaze landed on a man standing in front of her. He was portly, with a protruding stomach that was notable even through his expensive suit. His hair looked as if it had been styled into perfection strand by strand. His eyes burned with rage that contradicted his smile as he stared down at her.

"Well, well, well. The great Damien Zane. Finally in my power once again." Condescension was obvious in his tone.

She said, "What's up, mate?" If Voltaic were listening, the infomancer would feed her information about her location. Since nothing came through, Danica figured the place was signal-proof.

He frowned. "That's all you had to say to me? Not, 'I'm sorry for ruining your life?' Not, 'I'm sorry for breaking our contract?'"

Danica shrugged and replied rather lamely, "It's just business, you know?"

Another door to the room was yanked open, and a man in khakis and a button-down dress shirt ran in. He waved the wand in his hand around the room, and it stopped, pointed at her. He almost shouted, sounding panicked, "There's magic here. It's him."

Danica summoned bands of force magic, slipped them under the handcuffs that bound her, and slammed it outward until they burst into shards of metal. Jilly flew out of her jacket as she jumped up and blasted the guard behind them with lightning. The man who had just a moment ago been mocking her ran through the door the magical had used to enter.

Danica snapped, "Jilly, follow him." She dispelled her disguise and wrapped herself in shields as the mage threw a jet of fire at her. Frost magic met it partway across the room and nullified it as she snapped, "Are you an idiot? You'll destroy everything in here." She reached out with force magic, grabbed an award she didn't recognize off a pedestal, and hurled it at the man.

It bounced off his force shield, and he countered, "You're the one throwing Grammys, idiot." He cast lightning at her, but her shield handled it with ease.

She advanced toward him at a measured pace as she tossed other loose items around the room at him as a distraction. She had her gun, which could end the fight quickly, but this was someone she wanted to talk to if the other guy got away. Putting a large hole in him contradicted that goal.

She threw a blast of lightning at his head with one hand and snuck in a burst of force magic that punched him in the sternum with the other. His shield absorbed most of it, but the impact was enough to make him cough and break his concentration. She rushed in with fists covered in force magic and pummeled him with body blows. In her experience, wizards often relied on their wands to the exclusion of all else.

His blocks grew frantic, then he missed one, and she broke some ribs. From there, her victory was assured. Every time he blocked high, she kicked his thighs and knees. Every time he blocked low, she landed shots on his torso.

Finally, after lasting longer than she thought he would, he tried to take a step and crumpled to the floor instead. She blasted him with lightning magic until he was unconscious, then took his wand. As an afterthought, she grabbed an electrical cord from a lamp, ripped it free, and used it to tie him up. "Wait here. I need to have a word with your boss."

/ CHAPTER THIRTY-ONE

Madden Wells ran through the corridors of his house toward the nearest staircase. He couldn't believe he'd been tricked. He'd laid his plan behind the ones he'd paid Moriarty for and had known he was headed for victory when Damien had gone to the jet. It had been child's play to arrange the welcoming committee of fans in Cincinnati, bait he knew Damien couldn't resist regardless of the danger.

Madden skittered around the corner of the staircase as he grabbed the banister to redirect himself. He huffed and puffed as he ran up the stairs. Physical exercise was not a thing he did often, and it usually wasn't a problem. He hadn't anticipated being chased through his house by an enemy.

The sounds of fighting below heartened him, and he hoped his wizard would defeat the intruder or burn the house down trying. Fire couldn't touch him where he was going.

He ran into his bedroom and stabbed a finger on the

button that retracted the wall hiding the safe room. He pulled open the heavy door with grunts of exertion, then stepped inside and slammed it shut behind him. The only person he would've allowed in here with him was his wizard, who was hopefully busy defeating the person who had impersonated Damien. The lights flicked on as the room automatically came to life.

He picked up the phone to check in on his security's response. Once his wizard or the guards automatically summoned by the safe room's opening cleared the riffraff from his house, he'd be able to reemerge.

Instead of a dial tone, he heard only laughter. A woman taunted, "Maybe pay for adequate security next time, moron. Your place was totally simple to hack. You're lucky the door's not electronic."

Voltaic's voice crackled in Danica's earpiece. "He's in a panic room on the second floor. Bedroom at the end of the hallway."

Danica angled toward the staircase ahead of her. "Anyone else in the house I need to worry about?"

"No. Maybe he wanted to get his staff out of the way so they wouldn't see his reckoning with Rockstar."

"Well, that works to our advantage." She climbed the stairs with Jilly on her shoulder and entered the bedroom. She pulled on the heavy vault door with force magic, but it didn't budge.

The man spoke through a speaker. "You'll never break in."

She countered, "My infomancer tells me you won't be calling the cavalry, so I guess we're even. Who the hell are you, anyway?"

"You should get out of here before my security force comes in."

Danica muttered, "Yeah, I'll get right on that." She used her magic to rearrange the room and stack furniture in front of the entry door to prevent anyone from coming in behind her. Then she created a force shield along the room's perimeter walls.

She created another layer inside, behind the stacked furniture, and devoted a piece of her mind to maintaining the two barriers. She sat on the floor, crossed her legs, and closed her eyes.

The man yelled, "A train couldn't move this door."

She ignored him as she reached for the well of magic at her core and pulled it up. Jilly leaned against her neck, and suddenly the magic flowed easier as if the dragon was assisting her effort. When she gathered a decent amount, she stretched it out to the door and used it to pull. This time, it shook slightly, but she was still far from the amount of power required to wrench it open.

She drew the magic back into her and spent some time breathing to focus her mind even further. It was a matter of when, not if. She dove inward again and pulled more power up. It was an iterative process, pulling what was available from her reservoir and holding it while she waited for more to become available. Like she'd told Zack, she had never worried about how much power she could access because she'd always had enough for the things she tried.

When she felt full, she tried the door again, and it moved a bit. Again, she told herself to relax and breathe as she waited for more to make itself available. It might take all day, but eventually, she would succeed. Time lost meaning for her as she pulled magic from inside and added it to what was ready to try the door.

After five cycles, she knew the next would tip the balance. When it was ready, she yanked the door and rolled to the side.

The man came out shooting wildly, but she was out of his line of sight. A sizzle filled the room as Jilly blasted him with lightning. The dragon did it again, then one more time as Danica joined her to look at the unconscious man on the floor. "Well done, partner."

Jilly landed on her shoulder. "Well done all of us."

Danica opened a portal to the warehouse and learned that one of Arthur's team had portaled Damien to Cincinnati. Zack and Alexandra came through the opening and helped her tie up the man behind the plan. They deposited him in the study, bound back-to-back with the magical who had helped him. Her desire to interrogate them had fled. This was the man behind the attacks on Rockstar.

Voltaic hacked the house's video recording of the attempted kidnapping and gleefully sent it to the local police. When she warned them that the first responders were near, Danica, Alexandra, and Zack stepped through to the warehouse and the portal closed.

Voltaic confirmed, "I've erased any footage of your faces. They won't be able to tell who you are."

Zack asked, "How did you do that?"

"There was a cartoon once called the *Animaniacs*. Three

lead characters. On the recording, each of you has one of their heads."

Danica laughed. "Not one for subtlety, are you?"

Voltaic replied, "Not when it's unnecessary."

Danica gave the dragon on her shoulder a pat on the head. "All right, people, this is an unqualified success. We eliminated the threat and saved Rockstar. This calls for a celebratory drink."

An hour later, after everyone had showered and changed, they gathered at a bar called The Hatchet. The interior featured rock memorabilia everywhere, from jukeboxes positioned along opposite walls to signed guitars in cases to guitar picks with band logos glued to the ends of the booths. A small stage stood near the pool tables, currently home to a microphone stand and nothing more.

They claimed a table in the corner, and when the server came over, Arthur instructed, "Whatever they want, it's on me."

The waitress, who wore black jeans and a Mötley Crüe T-shirt, laughed and quipped, "So, steak and champagne, everyone?"

The comment earned a round of laughs. Danica was the first to order. "Hamburger, medium well, cheese, and like four orders of fries."

The waitress laughed again. "Got it."

Jilly appeared on Danica's shoulder and requested, "Honey. And berries."

The waitress wrote on her pad. "You're beautiful. I will definitely hook you up."

Jilly gave her happy wing flutter. "Thank you."

Zack requested, "I'll have what Danica is having, but just one order of fries."

Alexandra shook her head. "You people. When you get the chance to eat, you pig out. I'll take that steak, medium rare, baked potato if you've got it."

"We do. To drink?"

Arthur asked, "Do you have a recommendation?"

She responded with a sarcastic smile. "You might have noticed the giant brewing tank in the back."

He nodded. "I did, actually."

"So, lager, IPA, or porter?"

He rubbed his hands together. "Porter. I'll take steak too, medium, fries."

Danica requested, "IPA."

Alexandra ordered the same.

Zack replied, "Lager." They looked at him. "What? I still have work to do today."

Arthur shook his head. "No, you don't. None of you do. You've done enough for one day. What about your infomancer?"

Danica replied, "We tried to get her to come out with us, but she refused. Said something about being an antisocial homebody. We'll work on her."

"Is she an official team member?"

"No, freelance. But I really like her. Even if she's not willing to work for us full time, she'll be our infomancer until I have a reason to change."

He frowned. "That can be dangerous."

Danica nodded. "I know. Potential for conflicting loyalties. But I have a good feeling about her."

Arthur shrugged. "That's good enough for me. Your team, your rules."

Danica laughed. "See that you remember it." She was distracted as her phone rang, and she pulled it out to see that it was a video call. Damien's face filled the screen. He pointed at her. "You stole my plane."

Danica laughed. "Well, I wanted to find out who was behind it all. What did you have against them, anyway?"

Rockstar scratched his chin. "I kind of broke a contract with them. Hired a magical and an infomancer to make all traces of it disappear. It wasn't very nice of me. To be fair, record contracts are like the devil's work. You sign away your whole life just to get that first shot."

"I've heard."

"I tried to be nice to him and the label afterward, but they didn't want anything to do with me. Although I guess he *did* want something to do with me, just nothing I was willing to give."

Danica grinned. Something about Damien made you want to like him. "So, we good?"

He grinned. "I'm a tough bastard to work with, and you saved me from myself. Yeah, we're good. You have front row and backstage passes to any show you want. You just let Seth know, and he'll hook you up. Thanks a bunch."

Danica panned the camera to show her team. "Does that mean VIP for everybody?"

He let out a loud laugh. "Hell yes, it does. When you come, I'm buying the drinks."

"Good deal. Rock on, Damien."

He pointed again. "Rock on yourself, Danica."

The call dropped, and she laughed. "Well, that was unexpected."

Arthur grinned. "Like I said. They tend to be mercurial, celebrities. If the success on this first mission is any sign, I think you'll experience it quite a lot."

The drinks arrived, and the conversation continued. The meal went perfectly through dessert. After seeing everybody home, Danica kept a hand over the sleeping dragon on her shoulder so she wouldn't fall off. Then she walked into her backyard to sit in her lawn chair and feel the presence of nature around her. She was dozing after moving the dragon to her lap when her phone buzzed.

She fumbled with it awkwardly and found a text message from an unknown source.

Danica Grey, congratulations on your success with Damien Zane. Be seeing you. M.

She stared at it, then turned her phone off and headed for bed. Whatever it was, she could deal with it in the morning when she had some of her brainpower back.

In another part of the world, a tall, thin man in a bespoke pinstripe suit lounged in what others might call a man cave and reread the text message he'd sent. His chair was an excessively comfortable and equally expensive leather recliner.

A high-end computer so sophisticated it wasn't yet on the market for normal people rested on his lap. Monitors were arranged before him on poles affixed to the ceiling, curving from the left of his visual field to the right. He could have accomplished the same effect with virtual reality goggles, but he preferred the freedom to move around and still see his screens without the risk of tripping over something.

Information flicked across the screens in an unending flow. To anyone who didn't know better, it would appear random. The displays were broken into three zones controlled by a complex algorithm. The first included things in motion that he needed to keep track of and specific future opportunities he had designated.

Things his unrivaled computer artificial intelligence predicted might become relevant to him in the near future filled the second. The final and smallest section contained mostly random content.

Right now, that screen featured an old movie, one of the earlier sound versions of *Frankenstein*. He'd always admired the film. Although ultimately unsuccessful in his goals, Doctor Frankenstein showed no reticence in doing what had to be done to accomplish them. The man shared that perspective, and his ambitions were far greater than the literary doctor's.

He had watched through hacked video feeds as one of the many operations he had in play failed earlier that evening. He had calculated that five teams would be enough, and his computer systems had concurred. When Madden Wells had added a sixth and attempted to hide it from him, the man had known immediately and allowed it to go forward because it didn't matter. His plan would succeed, or it wouldn't. Then Wells' plan would happen, or it wouldn't.

He had already been aware of Spellbound Security. In the past, he had declined operations because of their presence. But his business was increasingly focusing on people of note, which meant he would doubtless have to go up against them again. The new office intrigued him. The others he saw as stodgy, like the company's owner. The two women seemed quite good for being so young. Their relative inexperience might be a weak spot he could exploit.

He would have to seek out more operations in their zone of influence to assess their skills properly. That knowledge would give him what he needed to compromise or defeat them.

He stood, set his computer on the table, and tugged on the knot in his tie. It was time to sleep since the sun was coming up. Every day involved meetings and decisions, and those things could change the fate of nations.

Moriarty smiled. The games he played were the lifeblood that powered his existence, and he anticipated with pleasure including Danica Grey in them.

AUTHOR NOTES: TR CAMERON

OCTOBER 26, 2024

If this is your first trip to the Author Notes, welcome! This is where I babble incoherently about things that interest me, and hopefully you. Those of you who have been here before, you already know what you're getting into. I'm impressed that you came back anyway!

I had a lot of fun with this book and am really looking forward to the rest of the series. Jilly turned out to be different than I expected, and I love her. She's named Jilly because of my ongoing obsession with Gillian Anderson. Ever since the X-files, I've been a fan. Ah, showing my age.

So, as is often the case, I've got a short story prequel to this book! It's Danica's first brush with celebrity. No dragon yet, though. It's yours in exchange for your email signup to my newsletter where I share EVEN MORE nonsense, and available instantly here: https://dl.bookfun nel.com/p3ilgsu5d9. If you choose to take the story and then unsubscribe, no harm done and I won't be offended.

The next book will be Codename: Scream Queen. I've also been a fan of Elvira for as long as I can remember, and while she doesn't appear in the book, the concept and character who does are loosely inspired by her. I remember back in the days of the dial up modem how excited I was to have Elvira sound files for all the things AOL (America On Line) said to me. "You've got mail" was never quite so enjoyable as when the Mistress of the Dark purred it from my speakers.

I'm looking forward to the Author Nation show next month. It looks like it has a lot of interesting presentations. I'm not able to stay for RAVE, sadly, as I have a day-job thing that conflicts with it. It might be my last one, though, which is sad because I've been to the 20 Books shows that preceded it all but one year.

The reason it might be the last is because I can only have people sub into the classes I teach so many times, and the kid and I might have an annual trip to Vegas in October now. We attended the When We Were Young Festival for the first time last week, and… wow. Just wow. A lot of people were wearing "Elder Emo" shirts, which I think makes me an "Ancient Emo." We saw WWWY Sideshow concerts on Thursday (Cobra Starship, 3OH!3, and Millionaires at the fantastic Brooklyn Bowl) and Friday (The Used, Taking Back Sunday, LS Dunes), a magic show on Saturday (Penn & Teller, who aren't as entertaining as they used to be – age catching up, maybe) and then the Festival on Sunday.

I've never been to a music festival in the crowd. I did some video work for Jamboree in the Hills back in the day but was backstage the whole time. It was something. 60-80k people. They were generally nice, though stunningly unaware of others as they moved around the festival grounds. It was like human bumper cars. We saw Carr, who we love, from barricade, and Millionaires again sitting in the shade in the back. Then we poked around for a while before finding a spot right next to the audio booth for the rest of the festival. We loved Cobra Starship and Pierce the Veil, Fall Out Boy (our favorite band) was amazing, and then My Chemical Romance ended the night.

It was entirely grueling. It was stupid expensive. I'm still tired after being useless for four days. But for the right lineup, we'll definitely go again. I treasure the time with the kid doing things that they love.

Before that, we saw Weezer (phenomenal) once and Twenty-one Pilots twice (first time great, second time in their hometown amazing). The rest of the year is slower, thankfully. We've got two shows in Pittsburgh, Pentatonix and Justin Timberlake (again). It's possible we'll travel to see a couple more. The kid is waffling about it.

We're caught up on *Doctor Who*. After watching from the ninth doctor on, that's a really weird feeling. We've started *Torchwood*, but it doesn't have the same level of appeal. I watched She-Hulk on the recommendation of my physical therapist and really enjoyed it. The finale was unlike any other. Highly recommend. Working my way through *The Penguin,* which is amazing. Each episode is like a present. Also trying to get through *Agatha All Along,* which hasn't grabbed me yet.

Nothing on the big screen holds appeal at the moment, which is sad.

Still working on *American Gods* in audio, as well as Scalzi's *The Last Emperox* series. Plus re-listening to Tom

Clancy books, which are like relaxing brain fuzz at this point.

I don't have a book-book at the moment. I finished James S.A. Corey's new one, and ultimately really enjoyed it. I also reread the first six *Sword of Truth* novels. Not sure what's up next, although I don't really have time to read at the moment.

Why, you ask? Because I still need to play *Baldur's Gate 3*, and there's an *Indiana Jones* game coming out next month, and oh yeah, a *Starfield* expansion, and next year the new *Civilization* game. *Civ VI* is an utter addiction for me. I had to delete it from my machine. I can't imagine what a new Civ game is going to do to my life.

That seems like sufficient babble for now. Here's the short story link again: https://dl.bookfunnel.com/p3il gsu5d9. I hope you'll join me for Codename: Scream Queen next month!

Until then, joys upon joys to you.

Standard monthly reminders - If you're not part of the Oriceran Fans Facebook group, **join**! There's a pizza giveaway every month, and Martha and (usually) I and all sort of fun author folks show up via Zoom to chat with our readers. It's a great time, and the community feel to it is truly fantastic. The group is very welcoming and enthusiastic. Oriceran Fans. Facebook. Your phone is probably within reach. Do it!

Before I go, if this series is your first taste of my Urban Fantasy, look for "Magic Ops." I promise you'll enjoy it, and you'll like Diana, Rath, and company. You might also enjoy my science fiction work. All my writing is filled with action, snark, and villains who think they're heroes. Drop by www.trcameron.com and take a look!

Your monthly reminder that you can find the free prequel short story for The Nomad Witch series, "Vacation Day," here: https://dl.bookfunnel.com/rxccsvm5jn

PS: If you'd like to chat with me, here's the place. I check in daily or more: https://www.facebook.com/AuthorTRCameron. Often, I put up interesting and/or silly content there, as well. For more info on my books, and to join my reader's group, please visit www.trcameron.com.

If there's one thing I've gotten good at over the years, it's reinvention. You'd think after decades of writing—being a journalist, a columnist, penning nonfiction about U.S. orphanages, and diving into the wild world of urban fantasy—I would have settled into a groove. But the truth is, being an author means evolving, and here I am at 65, reinventing myself again, this time with a new name. You can call me *Martha Roo* now. And honestly? It's about time.

This latest reinvention isn't just about switching up my pen name (though there's plenty of fun in that, too). It's about finally trusting my gut and embracing who I really am, stepping out front and letting my true voice shine. After years of telling other people's stories, some heart-warming, some heartbreaking, I've learned how important authenticity can be in every area of my life.

Let's back up a little. I've spent the better part of my life writing—first as a journalist, chasing down facts and crafting stories that needed telling. I honed my skills, figured out how to keep people engaged, and covered topics that mattered, including the tough world of U.S. foster care and orphanages. That experience was inspiring and shaped the way I see the world. It was important work, no doubt about it, but over time, I felt a pull toward something different, something more creative and free.

That's when I made the leap into urban fantasy. Writing in this genre felt like opening a door to a whole new realm —one where I could set my own rules and let my imagination run wild. Witches, gnomes, magical bounty hunters—I created worlds where anything was possible. But here's the thing: even though I was crafting these magical stories, I was still holding back in real life. I wasn't fully trusting myself, wasn't allowing myself to be fully seen. That quiet little voice inside kept whispering, "Why are you still hiding?"

That's when the idea of stepping out on my own started to take root. After years of writing under my full, name, I wanted something new—something that felt lighter, more fun, and, well, a little more me. Enter *Martha Roo*. And the best part? The name Roo came about almost by accident.

One day, while Mike (my partner) and I were talking about middle names and reinvention, he jokingly suggested, "Why not call yourself Roo? You know, like the kangaroo from *Winnie the Pooh*." He was expecting me to laugh it off and move on, but instead, something clicked. I loved it. *Roo*—playful, bouncy, and full of optimism. Everything Randolph (my old middle name) wasn't. I looked at Mike and said, "You know what? I'm doing it."

Mike, bless him, was surprised. "Wait, what? You're serious?"

Oh, I was serious. Roo was exactly what I needed. It felt

like shedding an old skin—one that had weighed me down for too long—and stepping into something new and exciting. Randolph had always felt heavy, like a name that belonged to someone else, someone more concerned with tradition than fun. But Roo? Roo felt like freedom, like a second wind at just the right moment.

And here's the best part: this wasn't just about the name. Reinventing myself as *Martha Roo* meant more than swapping out a middle name. It meant finally trusting myself—really trusting my gut—and deciding that it was okay to stand out front. After years of writing for others, telling important stories but always staying a little in the background, it was time to put myself out there in a way I hadn't before.

Sure, it's a little scary. Reinvention always is. But it's also thrilling. I'm still writing urban fantasy, still creating magical worlds, but this time I'm doing it on my own terms. It's different now. There's a lightness, a bounce in my step that comes from knowing I'm doing this for *me*, not because it's what's expected or what I've always done.

And what's funny is that, now that I've made this change, I can't believe I didn't do it sooner. Reinvention isn't just for when you're starting out in life or when you hit a rough patch. It's for anytime you feel that little spark inside that says, "It's time to shake things up." And here I am, at 65, shaking things up once again.

I've learned that reinvention doesn't mean erasing the past—it means building on everything I've experienced and choosing a new direction. All those years as a journalist, a columnist, writing about the foster care system and orphanages? They're part of my story, and they shaped the writer I am today. But now, as *Martha Roo*, I'm starting a few new trilogies, while still hanging out at Oriceran turning out a few new stories here as well. Keep an eye out for the newest Berens on the block.

In the meantime, here's to reinvention, to trusting your gut, and to not being afraid to stand out front. Whether you're 25 or 65, it's never too late to make a change, to step into your own light, and to embrace the joy that comes from being fully, authentically you. More adventures to follow.

OTHER SERIES FROM T.R. CAMERON

Urban Fantasy
(with Martha Carr and Michael Anderle)

Federal Agents of Magic (8 book series)
Scions of Magic (8 book series)
Magic City Chronicles (8 book series)
Rogue Agents of Magic (8 book series)
Witch Warrior (12 book series)
Secret Agent Witch (8 book series)
The Nomad Witch (8 book series)

Science Fiction
(with Martha Carr and Michael Anderle)

Azophi Academy (4 book series)

OTHER BOOKS BY JUDITH BERENS

OTHER BOOKS BY MARTHA CARR

JOIN THE ORICERAN UNIVERSE FAN GROUP ON FACEBOOK!

CONNECT WITH THE AUTHORS

TR Cameron Social

Website: www.trcameron.com

Facebook: https://www.facebook.com/
AuthorTRCameron

Martha Carr Social

Website: http://www.marthacarr.com

Facebook: https://www.facebook.com/groups/
MarthaCarrFans/

Michael Anderle Social

Website: http://lmbpn.com

Email List: https://michael.beehiiv.com/

https://www.facebook.com/LMBPNPublishing

https://twitter.com/MichaelAnderle

https://www.instagram.com/lmbpn_publishing/

https://www.bookbub.com/authors/michael-anderle